Summer of Stolen Secrets

JULIE STERNBERG

VIKING

VIKING

An imprint of Penguin Random House LLC, New York

First published in the United States of America by Viking,
an imprint of Penguin Random House LLC, 2021.

Visit us online at penguinrandomhouse.com.

Library of Congress Cataloging-in-Publication Data is available.

Book manufactured in Canada

ISBN 9780593203644

1 3 5 7 9 10 8 6 4 2

Design by Opal Roengchai
Text set in ITC Veljovic Std

For Lea, of course

I'm sorry.

That's what I'm sitting here thinking, Safta. I'm so sorry, and I want to make things right.

It's strange. My whole life until now I would've said *you* should apologize to *me*. And practically everyone would've agreed. Until I came to Baton Rouge a few weeks ago, you acted as if I didn't exist. I never once received a phone call from you, not even on my birthday. No letters, either. No cards, no emails, no texts, no presents. And you're my *grandmother*.

Now I'm in the wrong, though, not you. I'm sitting on the yellow linoleum floor of your storeroom, across from the boxes filled with your secrets, wanting to guard them. I shouldn't know those secrets. I feel so bad about the way I uncovered them.

I can't fix that, but I can at least try to understand you better, and tell you more about me. Things I never talk about.

I just have to decide how to begin.

Here's something practically no one knows: I almost didn't go to Baton Rouge. I almost stayed home in Manhattan, the way I have every other summer my whole life. If Ruthie Dane and Amelia Ogden hadn't turned mean about a month ago, in May, just before the three of us finished seventh grade, I would've gone to a bookmaking camp in the West Village with the two of them in June, then tennis camp in Central Park in July. I'd already signed up and everything.

But they did turn mean. Mysteriously and thoroughly mean.

It started on a Friday, the day before Hannah Arnstein's bat mitzvah. (I know what you'd say, Safta, if you were standing right here. You'd say, "You must have a bat mitzvah, Catarina." But wait until you hear about this one.)

That Friday, they were mean from the instant they saw me, right outside Spanish class. We were the only three girls in that class. Every day for months we had met in the hall before the bell, then walked into the room together. I always got there first because I'm in Math A, which is only one floor up. They're in Math B, which is three floors down.

You're probably wondering, *Math A? Does that mean you're better at math than they are?* Yes, it does. I am better at math than both of them put together. In lower school, when we had math classes together, I was always about fifteen folders ahead of them. That's not nice to say, but it's true. Plus, they were not nice to me first.

Anyway, on the day they turned mean I was watching for them to come through the door to the stairwell together, then wave and hurry over to me. Since that's what they usually did.

Instead, this time, they came through the door, stopped really dramatically, then Ruthie pointed at me and said, "There's Cat! *Run!*"

Then they both *ran* from me, down the long hallway!

I felt pretty frozen, standing there watching their backs as they laughed and scooted around anyone standing in their way. *Is that a joke?* I kept thinking. *It must be a joke. That's why they're laughing.*

I had a bad feeling they were laughing *at* me, even though that made no sense. I couldn't just stand there waiting for them to come back and laugh in my face, so I picked my backpack up off the hall floor—it felt heavier than it ever had in my whole life—and I went to sit down in Spanish.

We don't have desks in there. We have three long tables instead, set up in a U that faces the whiteboard, with a bunch of chairs at the tables. There're only eight kids in the class, and way too many chairs, and we don't have assigned seats. (I'm giving all these chair details for a reason—don't get impatient.)

I was the only person in the whole classroom at that point. I sat in a random chair and pulled a book out of my backpack, any book at all, I didn't even notice what it was, and I started pretending to read. I didn't want to just sit there doing nothing—that would've looked really weird. But I couldn't actually concentrate on a book because I kept hearing Ruthie in my head saying, *There's Cat! Run!* Over and over.

The first kid who came in was this boy Max van Helmond, who started at our school in sixth grade. I barely knew him because we hadn't been in any other classes together. I still thought of him as a new kid. Plus he's pretty funny-looking. His hair's frizzy and covers his eyes, and his skin is very pale—even paler than mine—and he's really skinny. I know looks are a terrible reason not to get to know someone. But I got distracted whenever I looked at him because I kept wanting to trim his hair.

Anyway, Max walked in and stopped when he saw me all alone. "Hey," he said, and I said "Hey" back. Then I went on pretending to read.

"Where are Blondie and Glitter?" he asked. That was obviously Amelia (her hair used to be white blonde, but it's getting darker now, just like her personality) and Ruthie (she's extremely fond of glitter—in her eye shadow and lip gloss and nail polish; on her notebook covers—she calls it her "signature").

I shrugged without looking up from my book.

"You're pretty talented," he said.

I did look up then.

"Not everyone can read upside down."

Turned out I was holding my science textbook upside down. I slammed it shut and shoved it in my backpack and crossed my arms over my chest and definitely did not smile. Max stared without saying anything.

Then Glitter Ruthie came in. *Again* she stopped and pointed when she saw me. This time she said, "You can't sit there. That's Amelia's seat."

"No, it's not," I said. And Max, who turns out to be a fabulous human being, said, "It's really not."

Again, there were no assigned seats in that Spanish class! We always just sat wherever!

Ruthie took her beglittered, freckly self off to the other side of the room and sat. Then she made a big show of pulling out the chair beside her and setting her backpack on it, obviously saving the seat for Amelia, who was definitely in the bathroom brushing her blonde hair. I didn't have to see that to know it. It's her favorite activity.

Max took a seat a few spaces down from me.

Then the teacher came in, and other kids, with Amelia last, her hair of course looking very freshly brushed and ridiculously shiny. She sped past me without even looking my way, and I decided I would never again trust anyone with particularly glistening hair. Ever.

Our teacher started talking about a new assignment—a presentation on Spanish artists. She never spoke English to us, only Spanish. As soon as she said the word "presentación," my heart fell even further, from the bends in my knees to the tips of my toes. That whole year, Amelia, Ruthie, and I had done every single other presentación together, the three of us.

I half paid attention to the rest of what Señora Alvarez said while keeping an eye on those two girls. I knew they wouldn't understand her—they never do—they're always asking me to translate. (They're basically not the smartest people on the planet.)

Sure enough, Ruthie started leaning over to ask Ethan Gardner questions. Then, when Señora Alvarez told us to break into groups and get started, Ruthie practically shouted at me, "We're doing this project by ourselves. The two of us."

"Well, then you're going to fail," I should've shouted back. But my brain had stopped working. I just looked down instead.

Then, from the corner of my eye, I noticed Max watching me.

"What?" I asked him, in a not-nice tone. I wasn't trying to be mean; I just didn't want anybody looking at me for a second. My whole body was feeling trembly.

"I don't have a partner," he said. "Want to be partners?"

I nodded without saying anything, and my mouth got all tight, and I had to take some deep breaths and tell myself, *broccoli, broccoli, broccoli* to distract myself from crying. Because other people's kindness sometimes makes me feel weirdly weepy.

I succeeded—I kept myself from crying. Then I *did* shout over at Glitter-Rhymes-with-Hit-Her and Blondie.

"We're going to be partners," I told them, pointing back and forth between me and Max. "And we're going to get an A."

Which—not to ruin the rest of the story or anything—we did.

As soon as I got home that afternoon, I went to tell Mom I couldn't leave the apartment all weekend. Ruthie, Amelia, and I had been planning to sit together at Hannah Arnstein's bat mitzvah the next day. We'd even planned our outfits. Ruthie would wear her brand-new, super-short, dark red, lacy dress. (She called it "merlot" instead of red. If you ever saw it, Safta, you'd call it "tarty." You'd call all her dresses tarty.) Amelia would wear her indigo tank dress, because indigo looks good with "merlot." And I'd wear my swingy aqua dress because, according to Ruthie, the aqua would make us "pop." (Ruthie always decided what I'd wear in these kinds of situations. I never cared. I know you'd hate hearing that—I know how much you want fashion to matter to me. But it's true.)

Now, obviously, I wouldn't be making us pop, because there was no us. And I wasn't going anywhere near the bat mitzvah, with them in their merlot and indigo, either. I just had to convince Mom.

I found her sitting at her desk, elbows up, face in both hands, staring at a sea of papers.

Her hair was its usual wavy, crazy mess, and I felt overcome with love because it's not even close to shiny. It's always on the dry side, and she tends to skip things like conditioner when she has a court deadline coming up, like she did then. She also zones out and doesn't fully see or hear me until I make her snap out of it.

None of that makes her a bad person! Or a bad mom! I don't want you thinking that, ever. She's a *good* person—she helps people fight for their rights. Plus when she makes an effort, she looks really nice. She never smells bad or anything, either—she always remembers to put on deodorant and brush her teeth. And she usually pays enough attention to me. Probably too much attention.

Standing by her desk, I waved both hands and said loudly, "Mom! Hello? Mom!" until she sat up and focused and smiled at me and said, "You're home!"

I made a sad face and said, "I don't feel good. I haven't felt good for hours." That was the absolute truth.

She got very concerned (see? she's a good

mom) and motioned for me to lean toward her so she could kiss my forehead. "No fever, I don't think. What're your symptoms?"

"It hurts here." I pointed at the right side of my stomach. She worries about appendicitis when I have right-side stomach pain.

The problem is, she knows me well. And I'm a terrible liar. It's a real issue. Right away, just reading my face, she could tell something else was going on.

Also, she knows when *not* to say anything. It's basically a superpower.

She watched me and didn't say anything.

"I'm *sick*," I insisted, gripping my stomach.

Not a word. Just a slight raising of eyebrows.

"It could be serious," I told her. "I've felt rotten since just before Spanish." I *had* hurt all over ever since then. "I think maybe I should stay in bed this whole weekend and just get better."

She finally spoke, getting up from her desk.

"We'll take your temperature and confirm you don't have a fever. Then we'll talk more."

We went to her bathroom; she cleaned the

thermometer—the whole temperature-taking process.

I didn't have a fever.

Mom leaned against the sink and started asking a million questions.

"Did you have a fight with Hannah? Is that why you don't want to go to her bat mitzvah?"

"No."

"What, then? A fight with someone else?"

"No." (It wasn't a fight. It was a massacre.)

"Well, was someone mean to you?"

That was a question I didn't answer. Because if I said yes, she'd demand details, and then she'd have a hundred and fifty thousand suggestions for fixing the problem. That's who she is—she fights to see justice served. I didn't want to hear a hundred and fifty thousand suggestions. I was confused and exhausted, and my feelings were hurt, and I wanted to be alone in my room with my pain.

"Did *you* do something mean?" she asked when I just stood there without answering.

"I didn't do one single thing!" I shouted. I *knew* this would happen—everyone would assume *I'd* done something wrong, because why else would Amelia and Ruthie just turn on me? But I *hadn't done anything.*

Mom shook her head. "No shouting."

I glared at her, and she looked back at me.

"I want to go in my room," I told her. Not shouting.

I can read her face, like she can read mine. I could see her decide it wasn't the right time to keep asking questions.

"Here's what I have to say about the bat mitzvah," she said instead. "Since you don't have a fever."

Then she gave me a whole lecture about how when you RSVP "yes" to an event, you have an obligation, and it's important to honor obligations, and each guest costs the hosts lots of money, and backing out is not the right thing to do.

(Doesn't hearing that make you like my mom more, Safta? Don't you think *you* could've made every single one of those points?)

Obviously my sickness plan got me nowhere. On Saturday morning I had to walk up the long, stone steps to Hannah Arnstein's synagogue all by myself. I wore a tan dress. You would've told me not to wear it because the color washes me out. But I didn't care one bit whether I looked good. I just didn't want to "pop."

As I pulled open the heavy wooden door of the synagogue, I told myself maybe Ruthie and Amelia had actually gotten sick and stayed home. Maybe God had stricken them with plagues and boils, to punish them for joining Team Satan. Maybe they had leprosy. Maybe their skin had started falling off in big chunks.

No such luck, though. Right away I saw kids from my grade, most definitely including Merlot and Indigo, at a section of folding chairs set up near the stage. The "bimah," I mean.

I'll sit by myself, in a back pew, I decided.

But then a middle-aged woman (you would've called her clothes frumpy—long cardigan, long blouse buttoned high, black pants) handed me a prayer book from a stack she was holding and told me, "You must be a friend of Hannah's. We have a special section for all of you, by the bimah." She pointed at the folding chairs and waited for me to walk that way.

She was smiling, but so bossy. "Go greet someone else," I felt like telling her. "I'll sit where I want."

Unfortunately there was no one else in need of greeting at that particular moment.

There were other greeters back there, though—at least three more middle-aged women holding stacks of prayer books. They all started smiling and nodding at me, too, all waiting for me to go to those seats. Like a frumpy army, ready to march me to the bimah.

So I gave up and started walking that way, down an aisle between long wooden pews. I looked all around, like I was fascinated by the building, like I couldn't care less whether Merlot and Indigo might be noticing me. Like I didn't remember *There's Cat! Run!*

The synagogue was weirdly super grand and shabby, all at the same time. Tall, stained glass windows, domed ceiling, crystal chandeliers everywhere. But also ratty beige carpeting and patches of peeling paint. Stains on the pews' velour cushions, too.

I reached the folding chairs way too fast.

Don't look, don't look, don't look, I told myself. I knew Merlot and Indigo were just to my right. *Pretend they don't exist*. But it was like they were human-size magnets, and I was a tiny paper clip. Of course I looked.

They were sitting together, leaning in to each other, whispering. *About me?* I wondered.

In the very *second* I thought that—as if I'd *shouted* it—Ruthie turned and looked right at me!

My whole wear-unnoticeable-tan-dress plan failed entirely, even though I blended perfectly with the ratty beige carpeting. I might as well have been wearing neon.

She made a face when she saw me, like I was maggots in raw meat. Then she leaned over and picked up her bag and set it on the empty seat beside her.

That bag was minuscule. Just big enough to hold a phone and her stupid, glittery lip gloss. But when she set it on the seat like that, it felt like one of those giant walruses at the aquarium, oozing over the sides of the chair.

"You couldn't have paid me to sit next to you!" I wanted to yell.

Instead I quickly turned left, then sped to an empty seat in the back, next to Layla Reza.

We're not exactly friends, Layla and I. But she's always nice, and she smiled at me when I plopped down next to her. Which was great. She's extremely quiet, though. Plus she's about fifteen feet taller than me—if I tried to tell her something, she probably wouldn't hear it, her head is so much higher up than mine.

So we didn't exactly engage in conversation. We just sat there, waiting. By the time the service started and Hannah read some Hebrew and wrapped herself in one of those big prayer shawls, I was doing some pretty deep pondering.

I know what you would've wanted me to be thinking, Safta. Something like, *Isn't it remarkable? Generation after generation, the Jewish people have come together in synagogues everywhere to read from the Torah.* You definitely would've wanted me to think, *I'd like to have a bat mitzvah someday, reading from the Torah myself.*

Instead I was wondering, *How can I dye their hair diarrhea green?* I came up with ways, too. Don't think I didn't.

I need to tell you something important, Safta. Even though you're not going to love hearing it.

I know you blame Mom for me not being more Jewish. I can practically hear you say this about Hannah Arnstein's bat mitzvah: "If your mother were Jewish, then you would have more of a connection to Judaism. And you would be saying the prayers instead of thinking about hair and diarrhea."

But if you actually knew what happens with me and Mom and Dad, you'd know that's wrong. *She's* always encouraging me to be more Jewish. *She's* always checking the calendar for the synagogue in our neighborhood; *she's* always hoping we'll go to events there; *she's* constantly asking if I want to be more involved. It's Dad, *your son*, who wants nothing to do with it, because he thinks organized religion tears people apart. Since it tore our family apart. Since you stopped speaking to him because of it.

The truth is, if you hadn't rejected Mom because she's Christian, and cut off all contact once Dad decided to marry someone not Jewish, Dad might've wanted me to have a bat mitzvah, too. And go to Hebrew school and High Holiday services and have Passover seders and more. If both Mom and Dad had been on board, no way could I have said no. Which is what I've always done, because when Mom did get us to synagogue, or when I went to other kids' bar or bat mitzvahs, or had Shabbat dinner at their homes, everything felt strange. I couldn't understand so much of it. The only Hebrew I knew was the name that we use for you: Safta, Hebrew for grandmother. Even that word seemed weird, since it sounds so much like "soft." And you are far from soft.

Anyway. My point is, you're more to blame than Mom for my bad connection to Judaism. If you see what I'm saying.

I don't want to talk about Hannah's bat mitz-vah party. It was horrendous. But it does help explain how I ended up in Baton Rouge with you, so, fine. I'll tell the story.

We all went outside at the end of Hannah's service and saw a slew of silver-and-black buses lined up near the synagogue, motors running, ready to take us to a party place downtown. I felt a powerful urge to walk right past them and get on the subway and go home. But then I heard Mom's voice in my head (RSVP, obligation, your food paid for, blah, blah, blah, etc., etc.). So I boarded a bus with Layla and sat beside her.

Fortunately Ruthie and Amelia were no-where to be seen. I'd bet a gazillion dollars they were in the synagogue's bathroom, reapplying glittery lip gloss and brushing their hair until the last possible moment. I knew they'd end up on one of the buses, though. If Ruthie wants something, she gets it done.

Layla and I didn't talk the whole bus ride, but not in a bad way. She sat all tall and peace-ful in the aisle seat, facing forward, her shiny royal blue purse on her lap. I looked out the window at parents on sidewalks pushing strollers and kids licking ice-cream cones and homeless people sitting on the ground, leaning against buildings with their legs stretched out. Other kids sat backward in their seats and called to one another, but I was tired of focusing on kids in my grade. Even when the buses stopped at the party space and we all crammed together into elevators to the third floor, even with someone's bag digging a hole in my side, I basically pretended they weren't there.

The elevator doors opened into a gigantic room, with food tables and games all around, a dance floor in the middle, and a DJ station with spotlights and speakers off to the side. The music was all *BOOM BOOM boom BOOM*, loud enough to make your blood shake. A couple of grown-ups were already on the dance floor, ducking and bopping; a group of girls ran out there, too, to the other end. I went to check out the food. I figured I'd spend the entire party checking out the food, even long after I was stuffed. Because food doesn't wake up one day and decide to set its purse on a seat to make sure you don't sit there. That's not the sort of thing food does.

There was so much of it, too! Taco bar, tapas bar, pasta bar, sushi bar, baseball bar (mini hot dogs, popcorn). Plus a turkey and roast beef carving station, a cheese station, an ice-cream bar, a cake-pop bar, and a chocolate fountain.

I realize now I should've been thinking, *All those homeless people out there, all this food in here, I should do something about that.* Instead, to be a hundred percent honest, I was wondering whether I should just go from cake-pop bar to chocolate fountain to ice-cream bar and skip proteins altogether.

Then Max, my skinny new Spanish partner, scooted up beside me, yelled "Hola," and popped a giant orange gumball in his mouth.

"Hola," I yelled back.

After that the lights came up a little and the music got turned off and the DJ shouted into his mic, "Let's give it up for *Han-naaaah!*" Everyone started clapping and the elevator doors opened and two men carried Hannah out—she was sitting on a big cushioned board with handles. She'd changed dresses after the service, into something toothpaste-green and strapless.

"Let's give it up for *Han-naaaah*!" Max kept saying, long after she'd climbed off her portable chaise lounge and was surrounded by people giving her hugs. The lights went back down, the music back up, and then all of a sudden two Agents of Satan—hair recently brushed, lips recently glossed with glitter, one wearing merlot and one indigo—were standing right in front of us.

"We're going to do our project on Picasso, so *ha*!" Merlot yelled at us.

It was completely bizarre. Why was she even thinking about our presentación at Hannah's bat mitzvah party? And why would Max and I care which artist they'd chosen?

Before we said anything at all, they'd both spun around and started running and laughing over to the sushi bar.

"Didn't Señora Alvarez specifically say *not* to choose Picasso?" Max asked.

"Those girls don't exactly speak Spanish," I said.

He nodded. "Right. I forgot."

He read my face—I must've looked pretty done with their mysterious and stupid meanness. He held up a finger for me to hang on. Then he walked up behind them, took his big piece of chewed-up, fluorescent-orange gum out of his mouth, and set it on the top of Ruthie's head. After that he turned quickly, flashed two thumbs-up at me, and hurried back.

That boy is very skinny, and his hair is like a separate living creature, and you're going to hate this because he's not Jewish, but I decided right then that I'm going to have to marry him.

The next morning—the morning my whole life changed—I lay in bed long after waking up. On my back, with the sheet over my head. I was wearing my honey bear pajamas, which I've had forever. You wouldn't like them because the pants hit midcalf now, and the sleeves end inches from my wrists. But they're very soft and comforting.

Never going to school again, I thought. *Never going to Spanish again, never talking to anyone again, just going to lie here.*

Then I heard my door open, followed by a few knocks, which made my eyes narrow, because what is the whole point of knocking? The point of knocking is *asking permission to open*. So knocking after opening is practically the same as not knocking at all. I've explained this to Dad (he's the one who does it) more than once.

Before I could yell at him, though, he said, "Oh—whoops! Sorry!" then closed the door, knocked again, and waited for my permission.

Of course I forgave him. I'm a very decent and good person, and it makes no sense that anyone would ever be mean to me.

"Come in!" I yelled, throwing off the sheet and sitting up.

"Mom got us breakfast," he told me. "You ready?"

I went into the kitchen in my too-short honey bear pajamas and sat with Mom and Dad on the tall stools at the island, and together we ate croissants from the bakery across the street. Mom likes almond, I like chocolate, Dad likes plain.

(Yes, Mom buys breakfast from the bakery across the street instead of making it herself. That doesn't make her a bad mom! It's an excellent bakery.)

I was nearing my last bite when Dad said, "I got a call from your aunt Miriam last night."

I have to admit, my heart definitely sank. Not because I don't like Aunt Miriam—I do! Uncle Bob and Lexie, too. The whole family!

But every time Aunt Miriam had called before, it'd always been to say that the three of them were coming to New York—would we like to join them for dinner? And our last dinner had *not* gone well.

"They were just here a few months ago," I

told Mom and Dad. "Are they coming back?"

"No," Dad said. He gave me a kind of amused look, like *I know this is weird, but bear with me.* "She called to invite you to Baton Rouge for three weeks this summer. The last three weeks of June. They want you and Lexie to spend time together. Obviously, that's not going to work for you—I know you already have camps lined up, and—"

He kept talking. I stopped listening.

There are plenty of points that should've at least flashed into my mind. For example:

Baton Rouge! What would it be like to go there, and see Dad's hometown, and the house where he grew up, and the family department store? Aunt Miriam and Uncle Bob were always mentioning the store at dinners, but Dad did *not* like to talk about it.

Plus—what would it be like meeting *you*, Safta? Because of the whole lunatic fight between you and Dad, I'd never laid eyes on Baton Rouge *or* you.

Also, Lexie. Why all of a sudden did Aunt Miriam and Uncle Bob want me to spend time with her? Did *she* want me coming out there? She'd acted pretty weird at our last dinner.

Those are just a few of the issues I should've considered before responding to Aunt Miriam's invitation.

Instead, I thought only this: *If I'm in Baton Rouge, I won't be at those camps with Tweedle Dumb and Tweedle Dumber.*

Dad was still talking. "I promised Aunt Miriam I'd let you know, but, again, there's no reason—"

"I'm going," I told him. "I *want* to go."

He gripped the island with both hands, like he'd just gotten high-fever woozy.

"Wait—" he said. "Why would you do that? It's a swamp down there—it'll be unbearable in June. It never occurred to me you'd *want* to go. What about the camps here? Haven't we put down deposits?"

He looked at Mom, obviously ready for her to say something like, "Yes, too late, deposits paid."

Instead she told him, with happiness in her voice, "The deposits are pretty minimal. And

I like the idea of Cat spending some real time with your side of the family." Then she looked at me and turned serious. "As long as you're sure you want to go?"

Seeing the two of them sitting there, watching me over the crumbs of our croissants, all concerned and interested—for a second it made me reconsider. Did I really want to leave them for three weeks to go to a place I'd never been and stay with people I barely knew, even if they were family?

But then in my head I heard the sound of Glitter and Blondie laughing. And I told Mom, "I'm sure."

I'd better talk about that dinner with Aunt Miriam, Uncle Bob, and Lexie—the one we had a few months before I got invited to Baton Rouge. So it's clear why I should've been worried.

It was sometime in February or March—whenever Mardi Gras fell this year. We always have our annual dinners then, because Lexie gets a week off from school for Mardi Gras.

In New York we do not get one half second off. Nobody ever says a word about Mardi Gras; I still don't understand what it is. I just know there are naked ladies involved, or almost naked, and people hurl thousands of plastic necklaces in all colors of the rainbow into the air. Lexie wore about sixty of those necklaces to one of our dinners, when I was seven and she was eight. She took off half when she saw me and set them around my neck. I felt like I was suddenly royalty—there were so many of them, in such bright colors. I still have them in a shoebox on a shelf in my closet.

On the day of our dinner this year, I came home from school in a good mood. I was still friends with the Demonic Duo, and Blondie had invited me and Glitter for a sleepover the next night. So I was practically whistling a peppy tune when I walked in the apartment. (I never actually figured out how to whistle, but you understand what I'm saying.)

The second Mom saw me, she told me to start getting ready. It takes about ten seconds for me to change clothes, and we had at least an hour before we had to leave, but I knew better than to point any of that out. Something about meeting Aunt Miriam and Uncle Bob always sets Mom on edge.

Instead of arguing, I gave her a big smile and told her gently, "Okay."

After that I walked to my room, plopped on my bed, and started to read.

I got pretty lost in that book. Also, I really should've closed my door. Eventually Mom saw me and shouted, *"Catarina Arden-Blume!"*

She only uses my full name when she's very riled up. I jumped up fast and started talking over her. "Sorry, sorry, sorry, sorry," I kept saying.

She was already looking snazzy. French blue

silky blouse, long silver necklace, black pants, de-frizzed hair, makeup, heels, the works. (You would've nodded approval, Safta—if she'd been anyone other than Mom.) She shook her head as I yanked open drawers and closet doors and pulled out a sweater, shirt, skirt, tights, boots.

"Your father's already left work to meet us at the restaurant," she told me. *"Hurry."*

Then she left my room.

A few minutes later she yelled, "I'm calling the elevator!"

I was zipping up my second boot. In a feat of perfect timing, I ran from my room, grabbed my coat from the hall closet, and sailed out our apartment front door just as she opened it to go press the elevator button.

I wanted to throw my arms in the air and shout, "I'm a star!" But Mom was still obviously annoyed with me. So I kept my star status to myself.

Soon enough I was cranky, too, because on the very crowded subway I ended up wedged between Mom and a large man who kept sneezing. I had to press myself further and further into her to avoid getting splattered.

As soon as we got to the restaurant I realized that Lexie and her parents weren't happy, either. I saw them the moment we walked in. They were standing near the hostess station, obviously fighting. Aunt Miriam was trying to hand Lexie a cardigan. Lexie, who was wearing a tube top, had her arms crossed over her chest and was shaking her head no. I heard Uncle Bob say, in a *do not push me* voice, "Put it on. *Now.*" So Lexie put it on, but she didn't pretend to like it. She was still scowling when we reached them.

Aunt Miriam and Uncle Bob noticed us and made themselves smile big. They both hugged me, which they did every dinner. It always felt a little weird, since I saw them so rarely. Aunt Miriam looked and felt tiny—too thin—and polished. Hair blown out smooth and neat, clothes unwrinkled, shoes unscuffed. She said, "Hello, dear," and gave kind of a distant hug, but I still got a big whiff of her flowery perfume. Uncle Bob was a huge mess compared to her, the way he always is—all those hairs coming out at the neck of his shirt and under the cuffs of his sleeves. Plus he's so big and loud. "How's our Yankee girl?" he practically shouted in my ear, as he pounded me on the back.

That's all the attention they gave me for a while. Even when Dad showed up, and we were seated, Aunt Miriam and Uncle Bob stayed pretty distracted by Lexie. All three of them acted weird. Usually Lexie spent a lot of time talking to me and showing me something she'd collected. One year she brought about a hundred scented gel pens and dumped them on the table; we spent the entire dinner sniffing them and guessing flavors. But this dinner she just glared at her parents and barely said a word to anyone, including me. She was obviously angry with them and couldn't possibly have been mad at me—all I'd done was tell her hi. But still. It didn't feel good.

Aunt Miriam and Uncle Bob were strict with Lexie at that dinner, too, and critical of her, in a way they'd never come close to before. Every other time I'd seen them, they'd acted like she was a unicorn with a horn of solid gold, like they couldn't believe they'd ended up with such a special being. But this dinner Uncle Bob took her phone from her, and Aunt Miriam kept telling her to sit up straight. Aunt Miriam even jutted her head in Lexie's direction while stopping Uncle Bob from ordering a beer (which was definitely strange—Uncle Bob always ordered beer at our dinners, and Aunt Miriam had never seemed to mind before). Like it was Lexie's fault he couldn't drink what he wanted. So of course I was thinking, *What did Lexie do?*

Then Aunt Miriam started asking me a hundred questions. "How's school, Cat?" "What's your favorite subject?" "What are your teachers like?" "Any extracurriculars?" "And your grades? Are they as good as they've always been?"

When I said, "I guess," to the question about whether my grades were still good, Lexie stood up fast and said, "We get it. She's perfect. A perfect genius."

I'm not perfect, and I'm not a genius. But before I could say anything, Lexie had pulled off her cardigan and thrown it on the chair and started walking away in her tube top.

Uncle Bob stood up, too. "Where are you going?"

"To the *library*," she shouted, without turning back.

Aunt Miriam hurried after her as I sat there, totally confused. *Should I not have said my grades are good?* I thought. *Why would Lexie care? She's in eighth grade in Baton Rouge, I'm only in seventh—what difference do my grades make?*

Then Aunt Miriam came back. "She went to the bathroom." She shook her head and laughed kind of awkwardly. "Teenage girls—you know."

I'd just become a teenage girl, and I didn't know. So I'm guessing none of us did. Obviously there was something weird going on, but after that night, once I'd settled back into my regular life, I didn't spend any time trying to figure it out. Turns out I should have.

I know I've already done a lot of complaining about friends and family, Safta. I sometimes think I shouldn't tell you any of it, and maybe I shouldn't even think it, given all the terrible things that happened to your friends and family when you were a kid. Probably I should just appreciate mine.

But then I remember, *you* definitely complained *plenty* about your living family. (Did you have living friends? I never heard about any.)

Anyway, the point is, if you could complain, I guess I can, too.

There's not much to say about the last few weeks of school. I started making bathroom stops right before Spanish every single day, so Merlot and Indigo wouldn't have the chance to be mean to me in the hall. I got the timing down perfectly, so I scooted into class as the bell finished ringing and slid into an empty seat next to Max. He always saved one for me, once we became friends.

The only time Ogre One and Ogre Two ever approached me again was the very last day of Spanish, at the end of class, after Max had tossed me a pack of gum and taken off. (He walked to school every morning and, on his way, stopped at the drug store for gum. Sometimes he bought me some.) I was leaning down to put my notebook in my backpack when Glitter and Blondie stopped beside me. I saw their feet first—they wore almost-matching sparkly sandals.

I slowly turned my head to look up at them—I'm embarrassed to say this, but a tiny part of me thought, *Maybe they want to make up before summer?* But instead of saying, "So sorry we got possessed by the forces of evil," Blondie tossed her darkening hair and started singsonging, "Cat and Ma-ax, sitting in a tree. K-I-S-S—"

I rolled my eyes and actually gave a laugh. "Shut up, Amelia." What was she, three?

"We know why you're hanging out with him," Ruthie said, one eyebrow raised. Like, *we are so onto you.* "But the van Helmonds aren't flying you anywhere. Ever."

I just looked at her, confused. She might as well have been speaking her version of Spanish—that's how little sense she was making.

Then she and Blondie walked their smug selves out the room.

Later I did a bit of research. Turns out Max's parents own a company that sells private jets to families rich enough to buy private jets. Which makes Max's family a whole different stratosphere of rich. Some magazine had just put them on a list of New York kabillionaires. That's why the subject was on Ruthie's twisted, tiny mind.

Obviously the kabillionaire thing matters to some people. Like Blondie and Glitter. But I'm not exaggerating when I say that I do not care.

I'm so very used to having less money than practically everyone else in my grade. We have plenty of money. More than plenty. I can hear Mom's voice in my head saying how unbelievably fortunate we are compared to the vast majority of people on the planet, we have everything we could possibly need and more, blah, blah, blah, etc., etc. She's right—I know that. I'm just saying, there are many kids in my grade whose families have their own drivers plus a cook plus a separate, live-in nanny for every child plus an apartment on Park Avenue (or Fifth Avenue, but mostly Park Avenue) with separate bedrooms for everyone, nannies included.

We have exactly two bedrooms in our apartment on West 94th Street. Zero live-in nannies, zero drivers, zero cooks. (By the way, you'd already have this whole picture if you'd ever visited, Safta. If you hadn't always stayed so far from us. Because of that stupid fight with Dad over him marrying Mom. I do understand now that it wasn't actually stupid. But still. It was miles from ideal.)

Anyway.

It used to bother me, comparing my family to a lot of the others at my school. One kid in our class has a movie star dad, another a record producer mom, another a grandfather who's a Supreme Court justice (we met him, in his robes, on our class trip to DC). I used to avoid mentioning my family, I thought we were so boring. Lawyer mom; finance dad; retired grandparents on Mom's side living in a little house in Idaho; Louisiana grandfather who died of a heart attack before my parents met; and Louisiana grandmother I never heard from, never saw, and barely knew anything about.

I wouldn't call us boring now, though. That's pretty much the last word I'd use.

I got more and more anxious as the day for me to go to Baton Rouge approached. A couple of nights before my flight, I lay in bed and thought, *What have I done? And why? I could've made Mom and Dad send me to a different camp here—like that baking class near Lincoln Center! I don't know a single kid in Baton Rouge, other than Lexie. And Lexie wasn't even nice the last time we saw her. What if she's mean the whole time I'm there? As bad as Glitter and Blondie? If she is, I'm calling Max and telling him to get in one of his jets and come pick me up.*

The Max plan wasn't actually comforting, obviously. For one thing, I knew he was traveling to Greece with his family in June. He wouldn't have access to his fleet of jets. Also, you can't pin all your hopes on a frizzy-haired, skinny, gum-chewing kid who bounces on the balls of his feet when he walks. Especially if your plan involves him flying a plane.

I got out of bed and went looking for Mom and Dad. They were sitting on the couch in our den, watching TV.

"I feel worried," I told them. Whenever I say

that, Mom gets laser focused, ready to help.

She turned off the TV. "What happened?"

"It's just—three weeks is a really long time."

They both scooted over, making a space for me on the couch between them. I sat and Mom put her arm around me.

"I understand that you're nervous," she said. "But your flight's in two days. We've paid for the tickets. You made a commitment. Besides, I really think you're going to enjoy this trip."

"I could call Miriam," Dad said, sounding perfectly happy for me not to go. "I'm sure it'd be—"

"No," Mom said, cutting him off. Which was a very bad sign. "That would be the wrong thing to do. Aunt Miriam has been planning for you, Cat. She's even asked me for a list of groceries to buy for you. You're going to meet family . . ." blah, blah, blah, etc., etc.

I barely even listened to her—I knew from the second she interrupted Dad that I had no hope. Usually they either agree right away, or they say they'll talk about it and let me know. When one of them feels strongly enough to talk over the other one and launch into a speech, we're done. I was definitely heading to Louisiana.

Sure enough, two days later, the three of us sat together in the back seat of a cab on our way to the airport. I have to be honest, Safta— that was the first time my thoughts fully turned to you. You'd crossed my mind, don't get me wrong. It'd occurred to me that I'd finally be meeting you, and I'd had flashes of wondering what that'd be like. But with final exams filling up my head, plus issues with Fiend One and Fiend Two, plus my worries about Lexie, I hadn't yet delved into the whole topic of you.

In the cab's back seat, sitting between my parents, I turned to Dad and asked, "What does Safta look like?"

He and Mom had been talking about something incredibly boring having to do with bankruptcy laws. Mom was getting pretty worked up about it—waving her hands, pointing a finger for emphasis. They both froze when I asked about you.

"Safta?" Dad repeated, like he wasn't sure he'd heard right. "You want to know what she looks like?"

I nodded.

He scrunched his eyebrows, thinking for a second. "She has straight gray hair and glasses. She's short. And she's very put-together."

"She is?" In my mind, your clothes were always rumpled and your hair stood up in funny spots. You had fury in your eyes, too. You were waving your arms and sending Dad away forever.

"Is she always loud and angry?"

"No . . ." He glanced over at Mom, maybe remembering that she was there for that big final fight, the day they announced their engagement. Mom smiled a little and motioned for him to keep talking.

"Safta can be charming," Dad said, staring into space, remembering. "Especially to customers. She can be biting, though. She doesn't usually raise her voice." He shrugged. "At least, she didn't used to. It's been a long time."

"Do you think I'll meet her?" I tried to imagine it. "Will she refuse to speak to me?"

"Oh, you'll definitely meet her." He was looking right at me now. "But don't worry. I've spoken to her and Aunt Miriam both. Your grandmother says she'll be on good behavior,

and Miriam promised to call if there's a problem. You can, too, just—"

"Wait!" I put both hands up to make him
stop. "You spoke to *Safta*?! You haven't talked to
her in fifteen years!"

"I had to. You're going to be living across the
street from her, and probably spending time in
her department store. I had to make sure she
wasn't—"

"Aunt Miriam lives across the street from
Safta?" I didn't care that I was interrupting
again. I looked from him to Mom and back.
"Why didn't anyone ever tell me?"

They both looked genuinely surprised.

"We thought you knew," Mom said.

"How could I possibly know?!" I shook my
hands at them. "You *never* talk about Safta."

"We have dinner with Aunt Miriam's family
every year," Dad said, looking apologetic. "I
guess we figured it came up at some point."

"It didn't!"

The whole conversation was making me
so mad, for so many reasons! I wanted to tell
the cab driver to stop and let me out—I'd walk
to the airport. No one had ever told me that

Lexie was growing up right across the street from you. Plus Dad had called you—his mother—for the first time in fifteen years, because of *me*, and didn't bother to tell me. He probably never would've told me if I hadn't asked. Would Mom have? Didn't she think I deserved to know? Obviously the whole "will Safta treat Cat well?" issue was on their minds, but neither one of them had taken the time to talk it through with me until I brought it up. And I was about to leave for three weeks!

I felt mad, too, that on top of having to deal with Lexie, who might not even like me, I had to deal with a grandmother (you, obviously) who didn't like my whole family. Mad that I was going to be stuck in the middle of a fight that started years before I was born.

It didn't even occur to me to ask Dad, "What was it like, talking to your mom again after all those years?" The cab was passing WELCOME TO LAGUARDIA AIRPORT signs, and I should've been asking questions or telling them I'd miss them. Instead I just sat there. Mad.

I guess being mad wore me out, because I slept through the whole plane ride. Before I knew it, a flight attendant was leading me through the New Orleans airport to Baggage Claim, where Aunt Miriam had said she'd meet me. The airport's way smaller and less crowded than LaGuardia, so we got there quickly. As soon as I stepped onto the escalator going down to the luggage carousels, I saw Aunt Miriam and Lexie standing at the bottom, watching and waiting. Which would've been reassuring, except for the way Lexie started acting the moment she saw me.

"Heeeeyyyyy, Cat!" she shouted, waving big. So strangely, overly friendly. "We're here! Right here!"

She was wearing the same sparkly sandals as Merlot and Indigo—I noticed that right away. They're very in this summer (which of course you know—I saw them in Ladies' Shoes, once I finally got to your store). I had on sneakers. I knew I would never even ask Mom or Dad to buy me those sparkly things. No way was I wearing the same shoes as the Beast Friends Forever.

I gave Lexie a small wave back, and she clasped her hands and bounced a little, like she couldn't wait for me to get down there. I saw Aunt Miriam shoot Lexie a funny look—one that said, *What are you up to?* So I definitely wasn't the only one thinking something weird was going on.

By the time I walked over to them, Aunt Miriam was smiling. She spoke briefly with the flight attendant, who walked away as Aunt Miriam gave me one of her pat-pat, perfume-y, *I'm not stepping too close to you* hugs. Then she asked about my trip, and the baggage carousel began beeping and moving, and we all watched for my suitcase, which luckily came really fast. Lexie rushed to help me haul it off, then grabbed the handle and started wheeling it toward the SHORT TERM PARKING signs.

"I can take it!" I told her, hurrying to catch up.

"I don't mind," she said in a voice that was still too friendly.

"That's awfully nice of you, Lexie," Aunt Miriam said. She sounded confused, but she didn't ask questions. She dug through her purse and put on a pair of enormous, dark sunglasses as we stepped through sliding glass doors and out into the heat. And I mean *heat*! It'd been plenty hot in New York, but this was a whole different, way steamier level of sauna. I felt like an oozing swamp monster had draped its cnormous body around my neck and was dragging its feet behind me, making every step nearly impossible.

But Lexie wasn't bothered—if anything, she moved faster. Her blonde ponytail was swinging and her sandals were slapping against the sidewalk and she just kept yanking my suitcase toward the parking lot.

"I really can take that," I told her, struggling to catch up.

She waved me off. "I don't mind doing things for you," she said in a weirdly meaningful tone. Like, *remember what I am telling you.*

Finally Aunt Miriam stopped in the lot and pressed buttons to open the trunk of a huge, fancy, black SUV. I helped Lexie heave in my bag (I'd packed for three weeks—it wasn't light), then we climbed up into the middle row of seats. Mine had been roasting in the Louisiana sun. I was wearing shorts and had to scooch forward so the bare parts of my legs didn't touch the practically flaming black leather. We yanked the heavy doors shut behind us; Aunt Miriam adjusted the rearview mirror; then we glided off.

"Music, please," Lexie called up front to her mom.

Aunt Miriam turned on some country music. I thought for sure Lexie would say, "Not country!" but instead she turned to me, all excited, and said, "Slick Billy and the Goatees! Don't you love them? We'll get to see them at the Bayou Country Music Jam—I can't wait!"

I'd never even heard of Slick Billy, and I couldn't remember the last country song I'd listened to. Maybe when we had a square dance lesson in PE? I just muttered, "Mmmn," and tried to look enthusiastic.

Lexie wasn't paying me any attention anyway. She was looking out her window, singing along to the music. Which was catchy, I had to admit. After a second she leaned forward and said to her mom, "Louder, please."

Aunt Miriam turned up the volume a little and started bopping her head to the music.

I expected Lexie to really get into the song

then. Instead, still facing Aunt Miriam, not looking at me at all, Lexie whispered, in a voice just
loud enough for me to hear, "I think we need to
go to the hospital."

"Wait—what?" I started looking her up and
down for wounds or signs of disease. "Are you
okay?"

Lexie held a finger to her lips for me to be
quiet, then pointed at Aunt Miriam and whispered, "Mom, I'm really sick."

Aunt Miriam was still bopping along. She
started tapping the wheel to the beat.

Still in that whisper, still watching her mom,
Lexie said, "I'm bleeding from the mouth and
ears."

It was a really yucky image.

Aunt Miriam just kept bopping and tapping.

Lexie turned to me then. "Okay. She can't
hear us," she whispered. I couldn't help imagining blood pouring out of her mouth and ears.
Why couldn't she have made up a broken leg
instead?

She kept whispering. "Tell me all about
seventh grade in New York. Do people have
boyfriends and girlfriends?"

I didn't understand why she wanted to know. What difference did it make?

"Some do," I finally whispered to her.

The whole couple thing had started in sixth grade. People would pair up for a day or two, and everyone would say, "Did you hear about blah-blah and blah-blah? They're together!" Then forty-eight hours later, tops, "They broke up!" Meanwhile, at school at least, they hadn't spent one more second together than usual. It all seemed very stupid to me.

"How do you feel about girls having boyfriends or girlfriends?" Lexie whispered to me.

I stared at her. Had the heat and pollution demented her mind? Maybe she actually did need the hospital? "Why would I care?"

She gave me a huge smile that actually seemed genuine.

"I *knew* it," she whispered, leaning a little closer to me. "Mom and Dad have this theory—I know how they think, believe me, plus I eavesdrop—they've decided you're all responsible and a genius and will be a good influence on me."

I still had no idea what she was talking

about. I must've looked it, because she started whispering really slowly, really enunciating. Like I wasn't a native English speaker.

"I have a *boyfriend*. They hate him. They think you'll steer me toward more productive activities. They're going to ask you to spy on me."

"They *are?*" I was getting mad all over again! Nobody ever told me anything, *not even the whole reason I was invited to this swampy sauna in the first place!*

Lexie was grinning at me again.

"I thought you might not know. I figured they'd think they could gently persuade you once you were at the house. I heard them say, 'What's the worst that happens? She comes, she stays, she leaves.'"

"That's the *worst* that happens?!" I wasn't even bothering to whisper now. I turned and glared at the back of Aunt Miriam's head. My only plan was to come, stay, and leave. And they thought of that as the *worst*.

"Watch and see," Lexie whispered. "They'll try to recruit you. But you're on *my* team, right? You're Team Lexie?"

One thing I knew, I was definitely *not* Team
Aunt Tricky and Uncle Deceit. "Yes," I told Lexie.
"I'm on your team."

I spoke too loud. Aunt Miriam looked at us
through the rearview mirror and said, "Everything okay back there?"

No. Definitely not okay, I thought, but Lexie
called up, "We're doing great."

We stopped talking for a while then. It was
really beautiful out the window—way fewer cars
than on any New York highway I'd ever been
on, and treetops rising up from still lake waters.
No buildings in sight. All the colors seemed particularly deep, the different greens of the leaves
and the blues of the sky and water.

A small part of me did appreciate all of that.
Mostly, though, I was wishing I was either back
at home or in Greece with frizzy-haired Max.

Aunt Miriam pointed out your house when we drove by it, but I only had a chance to take in a few details. I remember noticing the red brick, obviously, the dark green shutters and front door, and that big tree at the side of your yard with the branches that reach out, out, out, then down, down, down. Some even crawling along the ground. I don't remember ever seeing a tree with branches making their way across the grass like that before.

Your house seemed small, too, especially in comparison to Aunt Miriam's, which is gigantic! It must be five times the size of yours. I want to say hers is pretty, like yours. It's obviously meant to be, with its pinkish brick and tall white columns, white arched doorways, and white balcony. But there's something not right about that house. It's too big for its spot, for one thing. It looks like it wants to pick itself up and start walking off, looking for rolling fields and some peace and quiet.

We drove around back of that colossal pink-bricked thing, to the garage. Aunt Miriam's phone rang as she was turning off her SUV. She glanced at the number and told Lexie, "It's your dad. Go ask Rose-Marie how lunch is coming."

"Come on," Lexie told me, as she started climbing out of the car. "Come meet Rose-Marie."

I followed and waited behind her as she pulled open the screen. Before she'd touched the back door, it flew open, and a very sturdy-looking woman stood in front of us, in a room with large windows and shiny wood floors. The woman had brown skin and graying hair, and her face was a little sunken with age, but her posture was perfect, and I wouldn't have tried moving around her without asking for permission. She was grinning at Lexie.

"I *knew* you were gonna do that, Rose-Marie," Lexie said. "I knew you'd be standing right there."

Rose-Marie was peering past her, at me, but she said to Lexie, "Why're you standing there holding open the screen, letting all the bugs in to bite us? Haven't I told you and told you? The screen door has a job to do."

"All right, all right," Lexie said. "Let me through."

Rose-Marie stepped aside to let us both pass and smiled at me as I did.

It was easy to smile back. "I like your accent," I told her. I loved it, actually. She had a quick way of talking, with drawn-out vowels mixed in. I'd never heard anyone speak that way.

"You like how I talk?" Rose-Marie said. "Mærsi. That's a little taste of kréyol Lalwizyan."

"Sorry—kréyol Lal—?"

"Kréyol Lalwizyan. Ask tô ti kouzin to explain." Rose-Marie pointed at Lexie. "I've taught her over the years; haven't I, Lexie?"

Lexie sighed in an exaggerated way, like she was pretending to be exasperated. "Wé, you've taught me some," she told Rose-Marie, before turning to me. "'Wé' means yes. 'Mærsi' is thank you; 'kréyol Lalwizyan' is Louisiana Creole. And 'tô ti kouzin' means your little cousin. Not that I'm little."

"You'll always be little to me, joli Lexie," Rose-Marie said.

"Now she's calling me pretty," Lexie said.

"You *are* pretty," Rose-Marie told Lexie, "but you're also being rude. You still haven't made introductions."

"Cat, this is Rose-Marie." Lexie waved her hand from me to Rose-Marie. "Rose-Marie, this is—"

"I know who it is." Rose-Marie folded her arms over her chest and looked very satisfied with herself.

"Then why'd I have to introduce her?!"

Rose-Marie ignored Lexie and watched me. "I'd know that smile anywhere," she said. I smiled again. It's impossible not to smile when people are talking about your smile.

"It lights up your whole face," Rose-Marie continued. "You're looking just like tô pær— your father—when he was a boy."

It took a second for what she was saying to sink in. She'd spent time with Dad when he was young. I knew nothing at all about him then. He never liked to talk about anything having to do with Baton Rouge, and I'd never even seen pictures of him as a kid.

"How well did you know Dad?" I asked Rose-Marie.

"As well as I know Lexie here. He never talked about me?" She looked hurt, and I felt furious at my dad, even angrier than I had on the way to the airport. Why couldn't he tell me anything? I was going to end up making nice people like Rose-Marie feel bad, without even realizing.

"He never told me anything at all, practically, about anyone in Baton Rouge," I said to her quickly. "He doesn't ever talk about himself back then."

"Well," she said, "if you have questions about tô pær when he was a boy, you ask me. I worked for your granmær—your Safta—for years, right there in that house across the street, just like I work for Ms. Miriam now."

Lexie got an *I almost forgot!* look on her face. "Mom told me to ask you how lunch is coming."

"I'm not making any." Rose-Marie grinned at the surprise on Lexie's face.

"Why not?"

"Your granmær called. She wants y'all over *there* for lunch."

Lexie looked at her like she'd just said, "Couches all over the country have started floating in midair."

"It's a Thursday," she told Rose-Marie.

"I know what day it is."

"Thursdays are busy at the store. Safta *always* works through lunch on Thursdays."

"Don't I know that? Didn't I make lunch for your mær and Cat's pær every Thursday they were home when they were children?"

"Why isn't she working through lunch today?"

Rose-Marie was looking at me again now.

"I guess she wants to meet joli Cat."

I'd like to be able to tell you, Safta, that as soon as I met you I knew I would love you. I'd like to say it was an at-first-sight bond. But it definitely wasn't.

Lexie and I walked over to your house together, after going to tell Aunt Miriam that lunch was at your place. She was still in her SUV, with the engine running, talking on the phone. (I feel like I need to talk to her about the risk of carbon monoxide poisoning when running vehicles in enclosed spaces. But I don't really have a "let me explain something to you" kind of relationship with Aunt Miriam.)

Lexie got her to roll down the window, told her about lunch, and they had another "but she works through lunch on Thursdays" conversation. Then Aunt Miriam gave me a funny, *I wonder what's going to happen to you now?* look. I'd already been a little nervous, but that look made me want to go back inside and say to Rose-Marie, "Would you mind showing me where they keep the peanut butter and jelly? I'll just make myself a sandwich."

I didn't feel comfortable enough to be that

much of a coward, though. I'd only just arrived. I had to go along.

Aunt Miriam was waving us away. "You girls walk on over," she said as she started raising her window. "I have to go in the house. I'll meet you."

Lexie rolled her eyes as we walked out of the garage and onto the empty street. (The streets in your neighborhood are almost always empty. Mine never are. Plus yours have pretty names. Lexie gets to say she lives on Azalea Street; I'm stuck with West 94th.)

"I'll bet you five million dollars my mom doesn't get out of that car," Lexie told me. "I bet she just drives straight to Safta's."

"But isn't it right there?" I pointed at your house, maybe twenty steps away.

"Yep," Lexie said. "She doesn't want one drop of sweat on that blouse. Watch and see. She'll drive."

Sure enough, we'd just reached the median (which was shady, at least, on that hot, hot day) when Aunt Miriam drove by and pulled to a stop at the side of your house. She climbed out and called over her shoulder, "Come on, girls," then disappeared into the garage.

"We're *coming*!" Lexie shouted after her angrily. Then she muttered to me, "Isn't she *annoying*? Acting like *we're* lazing around, when we're the ones *making an effort*."

Aunt Miriam hadn't actually annoyed me— to me, her "come on, girls" sounded like "follow me!"—but it felt nice hearing Lexie say "we" this and "we" that. So I said, "Mmn," and nodded.

She liked that. She looked as if she might throw an arm around me, if it wasn't so hot and sticky. "*Wait* until I tell you what she did to me a few weeks ago," she said. "She and Dad both. Not now, though." She lowered her voice. "They'll be able to hear us."

We'd just stepped into your cool, spotless, concrete garage. It was mostly filled with that boxy, navy Cadillac of yours that goes on forever. I knew right away it had to be ancient, even though it was so clean and polished. Nobody has an extra-long, boxy car like that anymore.

"Smell!" Lexie told me. At first I thought she meant the car, which seemed weird. But then it hit me for the first time, standing there in your garage—the heart-stoppingly delicious smell of your fried chicken.

I got this really homey image of you then, holding a platter of crispy chicken toward me and saying, with a warm smile, "Cat! I made this special for you; I sure hope you like chicken. And I hope you'll visit all the time, now that you're finally here." Obviously that image wasn't consistent with the way Dad had always described you. But he'd kept other things from me—your recent conversation with him, for example, and the fact that you lived across the street from Aunt Miriam. Maybe he'd neglected to mention your kindness, too.

Then, standing near Lexie in the garage, I heard your actual voice, with its faint German accent, for the first time. I easily guessed it was you. I knew you'd left Germany when you were a girl. That was pretty much all I knew about your childhood—it was basically all *anyone* knew, according to Dad. Which is a little mind-blowing to think about. Would you ever have shared that critical part of your life story, if I hadn't forced my way into the storeroom with the yellow linoleum floor?

Anyway. In the garage, I heard you talking

clearly. The back door was open, a few feet ahead of us and off to the side.

"I called your home, Miriam," you were saying. "I spoke with Rose-Marie. I told her to stop cooking, you would come to me with Catarina. What is the problem?"

It was funny, hearing you say my name. My full name especially. Everyone called me Cat, except my parents when they're angry. I liked the way you said it, with your accent. It sounded European—musical and different.

"All those salad fixings I bought might turn." Aunt Miriam sounded a little pouty. "And I could've told Bob. He would've joined us."

"Bob does not need fried chicken. Feed him salad later. And let him stay at work now. That store of his needs more of his time, not—"

Lexie must've had enough of hearing you bad-mouth her dad. She rushed to the screen door, yanked it open, and sang out, "Safta! Look who I brought!"

Then she waved me forward. I felt mad at her for doing that, and scared, too. I didn't want to be introduced to you while you were

squabbling with somebody else. I didn't want
all that attention on me, either. And I didn't
want the weight of some big, meaningful moment smacking full force into me.

But more than any of that, I felt the pull of
meeting you. So I walked forward, and I looked
from your darkened, gray garage into your
bright, white kitchen, and I saw you. Standing
near the stove in front of a sizzling cast-iron pan.
Wearing an apron over your red shift dress with
the white piping. Holding high a set of tongs
and staring back at me.

You didn't even smile, much less say you'd
made chicken just for me. You were meeting
me, one of your only two grandchildren, for the
first time in my whole life, and you didn't smile
or say a single word. Your eyes squinted at me
behind those silver-rimmed glasses, and I could
practically see your mind working behind them.
Making judgments about everything about me,
from top to bottom.

I got annoyed, watching you assess me without smiling. I crossed my arms. I was *not* going
to say hi first. No way. It wasn't my fault we'd
never met.

We were both quiet for what seemed like forever. I have no idea how Lexie and Aunt Miriam were reacting; I wasn't paying attention to them at all. Finally you said, "I must teach you about clothes. Your shorts ride too low and your top is the wrong color for you. It washes you out."

I looked down at my shorts—which fit like the shorts of plenty of other girls I knew—and my top, which was one of my favorites. A sleeveless blouse, cream with sky-blue embroidered dots. I'd worn it special for the trip, to look nice when I got to Baton Rouge.

I had a flash of feeling embarrassed, for not wearing the right things. But it was only a flash. After that I got mad. At you. Maybe madder than I've ever been at anyone.

That's the very first thing you want to say to me in my whole entire life? I thought. *That I need to learn how to dress?*

Of course Dad stopped talking to you, I also thought. *You're nasty and mean.*

I looked over my shoulder, considering ways to escape.

Lexie must've guessed what I was thinking.

She grabbed my hand and pulled me into the kitchen and hissed in my ear, "That's just the way she is—ignore it."

Meanwhile Aunt Miriam was defending me. Which was very nice of her. "There's nothing wrong with Cat's shorts," she told you. "Look— Lexie's hit in the same spot."

"I don't like the way Lexie dresses, either." You weren't looking at me anymore. You had your tongs in the skillet, and you were flipping chicken.

"We buy her clothes at your store!" Aunt Miriam threw up her hands and shook her head, but she was half laughing, and I heard her mutter something like, "Just impossible."

"Of course you buy them there—where else?" you said, lifting chicken out of the pan and onto a paper-towel-covered platter. "I stock the clothes that customers want to buy. That doesn't mean we should wear them in my family. I stock men's underwear. Does Lexie also wear men's underwear?"

Lexie was pulling me toward a doorway to your hall, whispering, "Ignore—ignore—ignore," as Aunt Miriam said, "Of course she doesn't wear men's underwear!"

That's how our first moment together ended. With talk of men's underwear, and me ignoring and leaving you.

I know you hate that Lexie makes bad grades and doesn't work hard at school or in the store. I know you've said, or strongly suggested, she isn't smart. But it takes brains to be sneaky and scheming, and both of you are truly gifted in that department. You proved it while we were eating that first fried chicken lunch at your house.

Before we sat down to eat, while you were still cooking in the kitchen with Aunt Miriam, Lexie wasn't being sneaky or scheming at all, just nice, showing me the back of the house. "I should've warned you she'd insult you," she said as we walked down your hall together. "That's the way she always is around us."

I wondered all the ways you'd insulted Lexie in the fourteen years she'd lived across the street from you, and what I had coming. We passed the little table with the telephone, and I saw the notepad where you'd written, in your neat and curly handwriting, "Dr. Bergeron" and a phone number, but I didn't pay that note enough attention. Then we reached the first open doorway.

"This used to be my mom's room, when she

was a girl," Lexie told me. I could tell. It had a signed, framed poster of a band called Duran Duran hanging on the wall, and twin beds with pretty bedspreads—white with tiny blue flowers—and a desk painted royal blue with a big bulletin board above it. Photos and papers and ribbons were pinned all over the board, some covering others. I stepped closer—a lot of the papers were school certificates and, like the ribbons, they were all awards for math: Excellence in Geometry, Excellence in Algebra II.

"You're probably great at math, too," Lexie said beside me. She sounded a little resentful.

"I'm not," I told her. Truthfully. Yes, I get good grades in math, but there's a kid in my grade named Tony who's already taking high school math courses—he's the one who's great at it.

"Is that your mom?" I pointed at a thin girl with long, straight dark hair, usually back in a smooth ponytail, who kept showing up in various pictures. She looked like a younger version of Aunt Miriam. Happier, too—in all of the pictures she was smiling and surrounded by friends.

Lexie nodded. "That's her."

It dawned on me then—Dad grew up here, too! He must have a room just feet away, with a desk and posters and childhood pictures and maybe awards, maybe yearbooks—a whole window into his childhood, which I knew nothing about.

"Where's my dad's room?"

Lexie hesitated and looked at me kind of funny, then said, "This way." I followed her out into the hall again. When she pointed into the next room, I understood that funny look. White paint, white bedspread on a double bed. No desk, no bulletin board, no photos, no awards, no yearbooks, no posters, no pictures of any kind. You'd gotten rid of every single sign of Dad.

I didn't know then what had actually happened. I thought you'd thrown away all of his stuff. Making it so no one could ever see it again, me included.

Heartless—selfish—vicious. That's what I was calling you in my head when Aunt Miriam hollered, "Come to the dining room, girls! Lunch is ready!"

By the time we reached you I thought my hair might actually catch fire—that's how hot I felt inside. I ignored how pretty you'd made your small dining room, with those silky place mats you have, and the cloth napkins ironed smooth, and your white plates with the blue design that looks like lace. When I saw you near that fancy wooden sideboard where you'd set out all the dishes, I said, super sarcastically, "I like what you've done with my dad's room."

You couldn't possibly have missed the sarcasm. You must've chosen to disregard it. You looked at me from behind your glasses and kept your face very straight and said, "It has a clean, modern look."

Lexie started pulling on my arm and talking fast. "Come on—get some food—it looks delicious—you've got to be hungry."

From the very start she tried to keep me from getting too angry with you. Probably because she wanted me happy in Baton Rouge, so I'd willingly stay and help her with her plans to sneak around with her boyfriend. But also—

and I really think this—Lexie wouldn't like anyone getting too mad at you. Even though you were mean to her, she was loyal to you.

I let her drag me to the food. You and Aunt Miriam had set so much out on the sideboard: the platter of fried chicken; those wide, buttery noodles; the salad; the cornbread; that bowl of creamed spinach. I realized then how hungry I was—I hadn't eaten since the flight attendant gave me two bags of mini pretzels on the plane. Lexie was piling her plate high, so I took plenty of everything, too. Except the creamed spinach. I'd never seen spinach creamed before. I took just a little, to try.

You didn't like that.

"Take more of the spinach," you told me, from your place at the head of the table, as I set my plate down next to Lexie's.

"I'm fine," I told you. Not in a nice voice. Still not liking how you'd gotten rid of all my dad's things and bad-mouthed my clothes. And insulted Lexie for years, apparently.

You didn't seem remotely bothered by my tone. "Take some," you insisted. "You will like it, you will see. My spinach is not like your mother's spinach."

I lifted my plate right off the table then, ready to go scrape what spinach I had back into the bowl. "There's nothing wrong with my mother's spinach," I said.

Mom's spinach isn't particularly good. But that wasn't the point. The point was, you didn't get to say one single negative thing about her. Not after refusing to even try to get to know her, ever. Or me.

"I'm sure your mother makes the best possible spinach," Aunt Miriam said quickly. Very nicely.

"I would eat a whole plate of it," Lexie added. "Two."

The whole room felt weighted against you then—no one was going to let you criticize my mom, at least while I was there. But if you felt remotely affected by that, you didn't show it. You got a *why's everyone getting so worked up?* look on your face.

"Have more spinach, don't have more spinach—it's up to you," you told me, with a little shrug. Then you dug into the food on your plate.

"Sit," Aunt Miriam told me. "Please."

I sat, feeling better after all the Aunt Miriam-Lexie "of course your mom makes fabulous spinach" support. Everyone ate in silence for a while. I struggled at first to cut the fried chicken off the bone, then realized that Lexie had picked hers up with her hands and no one was minding. So I picked mine up, too. I was about halfway through that chicken breast when you set down your fork and knife and announced, "I think the girls should spend mornings at the store while Catarina is here."

Even though I was definitely still unhappy with you, I didn't actually mind that idea. I knew Dad had loved the store, and I wanted to see it. Lexie obviously minded, though. She dropped her chicken on her plate and started shaking her head at her mom.

Aunt Miriam's attention was all on you.

"You mean you want them to work in the store?" she asked.

"Of course work. What else would they do?"

Oh, I thought. Did I want to *work* in the

store? What would I even do? I had a vision of myself behind a counter, smiling at customers, taking their credit cards, neatly boxing up their items. That could be fun.

But Lexie started kicking me under the table, hard, and when I looked at her, she gave her head an adamant shake: *No.* So I focused on eating my chicken and didn't endorse the work plan in any way.

You were watching us both, and I expected you to ask Lexie something like, "What is so bad about working for me?" But you just speared noodles with your fork.

"Think about it," you said eventually. "We have time."

"We will," Aunt Miriam said. "I think it'd be nice for you to see what it's like to work in the store, Cat. Your dad and I both started working there on Saturdays when we were five, and we always worked there in the summers. Lexie did, too, one summer."

Lexie kept her eyes on her plate, but I saw her widen them in a look that said, *One and only one.*

We all turned back to eating again. I was

very aware of the sound of my own chewing, and the clinking of forks and knives on plates.

Then, out of the blue, you asked, "Do girls in New York sneak into boys' cars while their parents are away, Catarina?"

"Um . . ." That was all I said at first. It was such a weird question. Plus I got distracted because Lexie had gone very, very still beside me. And Aunt Miriam was looking pretty startled.

You kept watching me, waiting, so finally I said, "People can't drive in New York until they're seventeen, I think. I don't really know seventeen-year-olds."

"It's fifteen in Louisiana, isn't it, Lexie?" you asked, while buttering your cornbread. "Boys can drive when they're fifteen?"

"And girls." Lexie sounded weirdly careful.

"Why'd you ask about girls sneaking into boys' cars, Safta?" Aunt Miriam said.

You chewed slowly for a minute, not saying anything. Lexie started jiggling her leg fast, like a woodpecker. Finally you shrugged and told Aunt Miriam, "I hear it happens a lot here."

"Where'd you hear that?" Aunt Miriam asked.

"On the floor of the store, from customers." You turned to look at Lexie. "You are a girl in Baton Rouge, Lexie. Do you think it is true?"

Lexie breathed in and out slowly. She'd made her face very blank. "I don't know," she said. "I can ask around, if you want."

"No need." You dabbed at your mouth with your napkin. "I feel certain that I know."

Lexie nodded slowly, then pushed food around on her plate and stayed silent for the whole rest of the meal. You and Aunt Miriam talked about expected thunderstorms and a sale you were considering running and something about deer decoys in Uncle Bob's hunting store. It wasn't until you brought out a tin of homemade butter cookies for dessert that Lexie spoke again.

"I've been thinking," she said to her mom. "Maybe Safta's right about working in the store. It could be nice for me and Cat to do that together."

"Really?" Aunt Miriam and I both said.

She looked astonished. I thought I might have a sense of what was happening, but I definitely wanted to know more.

You showed no surprise whatsoever. You

just brushed a few crumbs from the table into a napkin and said, "I'm glad to hear it. Come tomorrow morning at eight thirty. We have to get Catarina better clothing."

Aunt Miriam's house isn't just weird on the outside—it's plenty strange on the inside, too. I got my first, tiny hint of that when Aunt Miriam was unlocking the back door for us, after your fried chicken lunch. As she was sliding the key in the lock she glanced at me and said, "I got the Duck Room all set up for you. Fresh sheets, fresh towels in the bathroom. I think you're going to like it."

I had no idea what she meant by the Duck Room at that point—I figured there must be yellow duckies on the wallpaper. That seemed cheerful.

"Thanks," I started to say, but Lexie, standing right beside me, spoke over me.

"She's staying with me," she told her mom, in an *I get to decide this, not you* voice.

Aunt Miriam shot her an irritated look, then gave a half shrug and said, "If that's what you girls want."

I actually would've rather had a private space. Plus I wasn't positive Lexie truly wanted me in her room. Maybe she did, or maybe she was trying to keep me with her at all times so her parents couldn't recruit me as a spy.

It made no difference whatsoever what I wanted—Lexie gave me zero chance to speak up.

"Open the trunk," she told Aunt Miriam. She was already walking off, toward the back of the SUV. "We'll bring her suitcase up to my room."

I noticed she didn't say, "Please open the trunk." Plus she still had that *we're doing what I say* tone.

I know what my mom would've done if I'd tried any of that. First she would've raised her eyebrows and said, "Excuse me?" Then she would've sat me down and launched into her "people we love" lecture. "Sometimes it can be easy to treat the people we love worse than everyone else, for complicated reasons. But I think you know that the kind of attitude you're showing is not something your father and I deserve. We don't behave that way with you, so you . . ." Blah, blah, blah, etc., etc.

But Aunt Miriam put up barely any resistance at all to Lexie. She just pressed the button to open the trunk, the way she'd been told, then called over to her daughter, "If only I could get you to bring your own things to your room, instead of leaving them everywhere."

"At least I'm not pretending to do stuff I didn't actually do," Lexie said angrily. "*Rose-Marie* is the one who got the Duck Room ready. Not you."

"I do plenty," Aunt Miriam shot back. "You think I don't do plenty? You want to do all the things I do?"

I'd taken a few steps back from her at this point. It felt like knives had started flying in that garage, and I didn't want to get hit. Plus whose side was I supposed to be on? They'd both been so nice to me at the fried chicken lunch, when you were so awful.

Lexie yanked and tugged on my suitcase instead of answering the questions about whether her mom does plenty. I couldn't just stand there letting her do that. I kind of pointed in her direction and told Aunt Miriam, in a calm and soothing voice, "I'm going to help with my bag." Then I basically tiptoed over to Lexie, and together we lifted it out.

"Be careful bringing that upstairs." Aunt Miriam pushed open the back door and disappeared inside, but we heard her shout, "Don't chip the wood on the steps!"

"Thanks for your help!" Lexie yelled back.

She grabbed the handle of the suitcase while I tried to find the button on the SUV that shut the trunk. By the time I'd managed that, Lexie was already inside. I caught up with her when she was halfway across the den, on her way to the staircase in the corner. She was still in a big huff, her sparkly sandals slapping against the wood floors.

"Did you hear her pretend to change the sheets and put out fresh towels?" she demanded. "I've never seen my mother change a bed in my life."

I was picturing Mom stripping sheets off beds, which I've definitely seen her and Dad both do, when we got to the uncarpeted stairs. I bent to lift one end of the suitcase, and Lexie told me, "I'll do it—don't worry about the stupid steps." But it was impossible for one person to pull that thing up alone. So we carried it together.

At the top of the stairs Lexie jutted her chin to the right. "My parents' room is down there."

I could see a little through the open door at the end of the short hallway—it looked kind of glow-y and spa-like in there, with the champagne-colored walls and sunlight pooling on the champagne-colored carpet.

"And the Duck Room is *right here.*" Lexie was already walking down the hall to our left and pointing at the first room she passed. "*Of course* it's the room closest to theirs. Aren't you glad you're not staying in there?"

She kept walking, but I stopped for a second to look in the Duck Room. Instead of yellow duckie wallpaper—which I infinitely would've preferred—I saw a big painting of men standing in a marsh, holding long guns, aiming them at ducks flying in the air above them.

That's not a Duck Room! I thought. *It's a Duck Murder Room!*

"I *am* glad I'm not staying in there," I told Lexie.

She was already pulling my bag straight down the hall, past doorways that I peered into as I followed. I saw a pearl-gray room with a queen-size bed. It looked pretty normal in there, until I realized that the wallpaper had a snake-skin pattern. I wondered if it was the Snake

Room. Then I couldn't stop myself from imagining sleeping in that bed with snakes slithering all over the floor, and not even a picture on the wall of hunters killing them. *It's the Living Snake Room*, I decided.

I hurried away from there. By that point I couldn't even see Lexie anymore. I called to her—no answer—and looked for her in the library with the leopard-print wallpaper and the shelves covered in leather-bound books. (Why only leather bound? I keep forgetting to ask. Also, I've never actually seen Aunt Miriam, Uncle Bob, or Lexie read a book—have you?)

Then I got frozen in the faux-log-cabin room across from the library. Because of the glass-front cabinets filled with guns! So many guns! I stood there staring—I'd never seen a real gun in my whole life, and there were about thirty of them, right in front of my eyes. Pistols mounted like dead butterflies pinned on a board, and a row of longer guns—shotguns?—standing tall in the next cabinet.

Of course I knew Uncle Bob has a hunting store with a preposterous name, Geaux Ammo & Camo. Dad had explained that in Louisiana

"geaux" means go, "ammo" stands for ammu-
nition, and "camo" is short for camouflage. But
even knowing that Uncle Bob celebrates ammo
and camo, it still surprised me to see so many
weapons in his house, just a crash of glass away
from anyone who wanted them.

When Lexie came in two seconds later, I was
pulling on the door of her dad's gun cabinet,
checking whether it was locked.

"What're you doing?" she said. "Come on—
come see my room."

"Are those real?" I pointed at the guns.

"You think they're toys?" She laughed. "Of
course they're real. My dad collects them. Don't
ask him about them—he'll never shut up. Eigh-
teenth century something, Revolutionary War
something else, on and on, who could possibly
care? Come on."

"But—" I followed her into the hallway. "Are
they loaded?"

"There's an ammo drawer," she said. Which
maybe answered the question and maybe didn't.
"The cabinet's locked, the drawer's locked.
Don't worry about it."

Don't worry? We were talking about guns!

Of course I worried! How could I be related to people who displayed them like they were fancy china?

I felt like I needed to sit Uncle Bob and Aunt Miriam down and have a serious talk. I pictured them perched meekly on the edge of their bed in their glow-y room, while I pointed my finger at them and said, "Stop running your car in enclosed spaces, and get rid of your gun room!"

Lexie turned into her room, finally, and told me, "This is us." She'd decorated the whole room in black and white with pops of watermelon. White carpet, white wallpaper with black dots, white and black color-blocked comforters on her twin beds. Watermelon beanbags, watermelon table lamps, watermelon window shades. No sign of guns, thank goodness. Or animals—except I did have a weird and not-nice thought about zebras and intestines.

"Look over here," Lexie told me, as I was trying to get *Zebra Intestines Room* out of my head. She climbed on her window seat and pointed. "See?"

I knelt beside her and looked. There was

a big deck out her window, shaded by the branches of a tall tree. To the left of the tree I could see your house across the street.

"She stands at that kitchen window and watches." Lexie was still pointing. Obviously meaning you. "I thought it was only when she knew I was on my way over there—she's always telling my parents whether I looked both ways when I crossed the street, even when it couldn't possibly have mattered because there were no cars *anywhere*. But I guess she keeps an eye on my deck, too. She must've been looking one time when I snuck out to see Hank."

I figured Hank must be the boyfriend, but I had other questions.

"How do you get down from the deck?"

She pointed at the tree. "It's easy to climb—you'll see."

No, I thought. *No, I will not see.* I don't climb trees. I don't like the feel of bark on bare legs. I don't like bugs. I like air-conditioning and bagel stores. I don't like the idea of sneaking out, either. I like it when grown-ups know where I am. If I'm going to get kidnapped, I want my mom and dad badgering the cops right away, telling them to find me *now*.

Lexie had no idea what was going on in my head. She was grinning. "Wait till you meet Hank—you're going to love him. Everybody loves him. Everybody who's not my parents. They hate him, especially since they caught us together in the cedar closet in Dad's store a few weeks ago. We weren't doing *anything*, but they went nuts. But they don't know anything about anything. It's been great now that he's fifteen and got his driver's license, and his parents gave him a car. A really cool one—you'll see. We'll have to be more careful about meeting him. Maybe he'll come sneak us away from the store while we're doing all that working—except Safta's like a hawk in there. We'll figure it out, though. Good thing you're smart."

She gave me a few pats on my shoulder. I barely felt them. I was thinking instead about the fifteen-year-old boys at my school, rushing through hallways in packs, sometimes jumping on one another. Never paying any attention to anybody in the hall outside their group, just assuming everyone else would step aside. None of them bothering to apologize, either, if they ended up barreling into you, or forcing you to press up against the wall to avoid getting run down. And that was when they were on foot! Who could possibly want them driving cars?

I decided right then—no way was I getting into a car with Hunky Hank behind the wheel.

Nobody was keeping Lexie away from him, though. That was a hundred percent clear. She hopped off the window seat and started texting him.

I did some unpacking and some reading. She kept texting. I thought way too much about death by gunshot and by car crashing into a tree, then bursting into flame. Still, she texted.

"Who're you texting now?" I finally asked her. By this point the sun was far lower in the sky.

"Gabby," she said, without looking up or slowing the tapping of her thumbs.

I got jealous. I wanted to text with a friend.

I looked at my phone. Other than with Mom and Dad, my last texts were with Max, about what kind of gum he should bring me.

Menta? Or fruta?

Menta por favor.

On the last day of school, he'd told me he was going to Greece with his parents. "Sounds fun," I'd said. He'd shrugged and said, "My mom spends the whole time bugging me to put on sunscreen." So I'm guessing she's a good mom. The boy is very pale. (In case you're wondering, the answer is yes, Mom makes me wear sunscreen, too.)

How's the sunburn? I texted Max now.

After a few seconds he wrote back. The ears are gonna peel.

I nodded.

So easy to forget the ears.

How's Baton Rouge?

Pretty crazy. Lots of guns in the house. Lexie's parents and Safta hate her boyfriend Hank.

I looked up, considering what else to say, and realized there was almost no light left in the sky. Which led to a bad thought.

Wait—what time is it there?

After a pause, he wrote, 3:12 A.M.

WHY ARE YOU UP?!

SOMEONE TEXTED ME!

SORRY SORRY SORRY. I felt terrible. Go back to sleep!

No es un problema

ES a problema! You'll fall asleep in the sun tomorrow and get even more burned.

Fine, he wrote. But keep me posted about weapons stockpile and bad news boyfriend.

I will.

Lexie was watching me when I set down my phone.

"Why are you smiling like that?" she asked. "Who were *you* texting?"

"No one." I hadn't realized I was smiling, but I was. "Just a friend."

She raised her eyebrows. "Really? Just a friend?"

"Really," I told her.

She smirked a little, like she knew better. Which was extremely annoying.

Before I could say "Just because *you* have a boyfriend doesn't mean the whole world wants one," she hopped up.

"Come on," she said. "I'm hungry—it's got to be time to eat."

You really messed up my head when it came to clothes. I could not decide what to wear to go meet you at the store the next morning. My shorts "rode" wrong, apparently. My jeans probably did, too, plus it was too hot to wear them—I could see the sun already baking into the wood on the deck outside Lexie's room, and no breeze moving through the tree. My skirt might be okay, but it went with a white top—did white wash me out the way cream did? What did that even mean? Then there was the coral sundress I'd brought in case we had a fancy occasion. Did shopping at your store count as fancy?

"What do you think?" I asked Lexie, holding up the skirt outfit and the dress. "Which one should I wear?"

She shrugged, still in her bed, still wearing her sky-blue short-set pajamas. She looked wide-awake, though, all pink cheeked and happy eyed. She'd been texting for a while.

"Doesn't matter," she told me. "She's going to buy you all new things anyway."

I'd already given the you-buying-me-things issue some thought. I didn't love the idea of you spending a lot of money on clothes for me, and I'd considered asking my parents whether I should let you, when I'd called them the night before. But then I realized—I was only getting the clothes because you'd decided, after seeing me *once*, that I needed a new wardrobe. Why should my parents pay for that?

I heard a weird beeping coming from Lexie's direction then. I must've looked confused. "Intercom," she told me and pointed at a box with buttons on the wall. One second later Aunt Miriam's voice came through it.

"Girls! Breakfast! You don't want to be late for Safta!"

Very true—I did not want to be late for you. I threw on the coral sundress and buckled on some sandals. Then I realized—Lexie had gotten out of bed, but she wasn't getting ready. She seemed to be getting un-ready. She was just finishing misbuttoning her pajama top. As I stared, she rumpled her hair.

"Listen," she told me, hair now covering a bunch of her face. "I'm going to need your backup down there, okay? I can't spend all that time at Safta's store. Hank's got his Piggly Wiggly shift; I can walk over and hang out with him. Mom and Dad'll be at work, Safta'll be all caught up with you, it's perfect."

I kept staring, mouth open now. I didn't know where to start. What was a Piggly Wiggly? And how could she leave me alone with you for a whole morning? "I need *your* backup," I told her.

She waved that off and tucked one part of her pajama top into the bottoms, leaving the rest out. "You don't want one more person in that fitting room, watching you get dressed and undressed."

"What do you mean, one more person? Who's going to be watching me dress and undress?"

I must've sounded pretty panicky—she took a good look at me then, pausing her plan, trying to figure out how to deal with my unexpected resistance.

"You should come with me to the Piggly Wiggly," she said finally. "We'll pretend you're sick, too, then we'll walk over there together when Mom and Dad leave for work. It's only about two miles. It'll be fun. We'll have to hide from the manager—Hank's not supposed to have friends there while he's working. But we can hang out in produce, sniff melons and stuff, and we can laugh at him—he wears this apron— it's really cute."

"No," I told her. "No thank you." I don't know whether she was deliberately trying to make it a hundred percent unappealing to me, but she definitely did. I had zero interest in sniffing melons at the Piggly Wiggly and giggling over He-Man Hank in his apron while an angry manager hunted me down. "I'll back you up with your parents. Let's go."

It was amazing, watching her finish her transformation between her bedroom and the kitchen. She started sniffling halfway down the stairs. As we crossed the den, she started walking all hunched and made her eyes dull, her mouth droopy. She actually looked paler. I could see her living a life of crime—she'd evade capture every time, without even wearing a wig.

I watched in awe as she rubbed her forehead a little and stepped into the kitchen.

"Good morning!" Aunt Miriam and Uncle Bob both sang out. Uncle Bob was sitting at the head of the table with a mug of coffee and a plate piled high with pancakes dripping in syrup. Aunt Miriam had a half grapefruit and a small plate of scrambled eggs. Their faces both changed from "Welcome!" to "What happened?!" when they registered Lexie's appearance. They fully bought the act—unlike Mom, when I faked illness. I'm not saying they're stupider than Mom; Lexie is definitely better at faking than I am. I will say this, though: Rose-Marie, standing over by the stove, looked plenty skeptical.

You can guess how the rest of that break- fast went. Lexie told her parents she'd woken up feeling terrible, she wasn't sure what had happened, she'd heard some friends had a bug, she must've caught it from them at the pool. She even pretended not to have an appetite, but Rose-Marie was having none of that.

"I made these biscuits for you girls," she said, giving Lexie a *don't you let them go to waste* look. "You know you love my biskwi. Bring those up- stairs for when you get hungry later."

"Mærsi," Lexie told her in a weak voice, taking the plate loaded up with biscuits and heading slowly out of the room. Abandoning me for the whole rest of the morning.

The drive to your store wasn't long, but it was a little creepy. We got stuck at that stoplight in front of the cemetery nearby. It's so old, that cemetery, with graves packed close together and coffins breaking back up through the dirt in a slant. I couldn't stop staring at the jagged holes in some of the coffin lids—I kept imagining a bony hand creeping out and wriggling its fingers. Just as I was about to say, "Go, go, go! Run the light! I don't care!" it finally changed to green.

"Almost there," Aunt Miriam told me.

A few blocks later we reached your store. Which is so pretty! That stone the color of sand at Fire Island, all those picture windows, the white columns on the wide patio in front of the row of glass doors, and your name in big silver fancy letters above them: GERTA'S.

I hadn't realized how big the store is, too! I'd known it was a department store, but I'd thought of it as having just a few, small departments. It stretches over that whole block, though, just like Saks and Bloomingdale's do in Manhattan. Obviously it doesn't have nearly as many floors. But you also have that second building,

just across the road, with the big sign that says
GERTA'S CAR CARE CENTER.

I'm not that big on history—it's definitely
my least favorite subject—but I did think then
that you'd had that business forever, and there
couldn't possibly have been that many women
with big old stores back in those days. Much
less car care centers. How many women have
car care centers now? Plus Mom keeps talking
about how many stores have closed because of
online shopping. Yours is still here.

As Aunt Miriam turned into the wide lot in
front of the store, I saw your navy boat of a car
parked on the sidewalk, all the way at the end,
even though the store hadn't even opened yet
and there were a million empty spots.

"Isn't that Safta's car?" I asked.

"She always parks there," Aunt Miriam
said. "She doesn't want to take a spot from a
customer."

I tried to remember if I'd ever once, in my
whole life, seen a car parked on a sidewalk in
Manhattan. No. Never.

"Doesn't she get a ticket?"

Aunt Miriam laughed. "Police officers shopped

here when they were boys and worked here while they were in school. All of the store's security guards are retired police officers. They love Safta. Plus, would you want to give her a ticket?"

Did that mean you could commit crimes? I got this image in my head of you inside a supermarket, shoving melons into a big purse. Then Aunt Miriam stopped the car near the patio in front of the glass doors.

"Here we are," she said. "Safta knows it's just you—I called already. I'll pick you up in a couple of hours."

I hesitated—she wasn't going to bring me in?

She was watching me in her rearview mirror and must've sensed what I was thinking. "Oh! I'm so used to dropping off Lexie. Do you want me to come with you? I can park—hang on."

"No," I said quickly. She was making me feel like a baby. "I'm fine."

I opened my car door and got out and closed the door very hard. "I've done plenty that's a lot scarier than this," I felt like telling her. It was true—one time on the way to school I had to walk around a dead body in the subway station.

The police had covered it with a blanket, head to toe, and put up yellow tape and everything.

I did weirdly feel more nervous about walking into the store than I had walking around that dead body, though. Mom had been with me then, and now I was all alone.

I watched as Aunt Miriam drove back across the lot, her car getting farther and farther away. It occurred to me suddenly that she hadn't even taken Lexie's temperature. My mom always took my temperature when I was trying to fake being sick. "You need to get smarter," I wanted to tell Aunt Miriam. She made a left out of the lot and disappeared.

I turned to go into the store all alone. And saw a young woman, maybe in her early twenties, pointing right at me from the other side of the glass door.

"Come in, come in!" the young woman told me, throwing open the door. She had a long body—long arms, long legs—and a short haircut that brought out her eyes. She wore chandelier earrings and a white sleeveless dress that stood out against her dark brown skin. The dress had an asymmetrical neckline and bands of intricate, colorful embroidery near the hem, and it fit her so perfectly—for the first time I thought maybe you were right, maybe I *should* care more about what I wore.

She started talking while I was still standing outside, admiring her dress, and it turned out she had a lot to say.

"You're Catarina, right? I don't want to let in the wrong person before the store opens—your grandmother would kill me. I'm Merry, short for Meredith, spelled M-e-r-r-y. Everyone thinks it's Mary, as in 'our Mother full of grace,' so I'm always spelling it. Your name's pretty—Catarina, like ballerina. How did your parents choose it? I've never heard it before."

"Um . . ." I needed a second to take in everything she'd said. "Catarina is the place in

Guatemala where my parents met. Really randomly, on separate trips one winter. Most everybody calls me Cat."

"Cat!" Merry looked like I'd just offered her a
cupcake. "How fun! Should I call you that, too?"

"Sure," I told her, laughing. She had so much
excitement in her.

"Come on, Cat!" She waved me in with a big
arm motion. "Come inside!"

I stepped past her, from the buggy sauna
outside to the clean, refrigerated-feeling air of
your store. I took a second to look all around.
It's so pretty in there, with the sunlight angling
through the big windows and all the colorful
clothes hanging so neatly on shiny metal fixtures, and the silvery carpeting with the white,
white walls. It felt quiet and peaceful, too. No
customers yet, no employees at their stations.
I could hear voices, faintly, but no one was in
sight. No one except Merry.

"I'm an assistant to the buyer for Juniors,"
she said, pointing to the department on our right.
"Just for the summer—I go back to college in the
fall. It's a great summer job; I get to flip through
magazines and watch fashion shows, looking

for trends. So fun, right? My best friend Clarice got too jealous when she heard that. She's waitressing—we're both saving up for a textile design program. She keeps worrying she'll drop a tray of food on somebody's head."

"That'd be bad," I said, imagining spaghetti and tomato sauce sliding down my hair, onto my shoulders.

"I know, right?" Her eyes got even bigger in her face. "I make mistakes here, don't get me wrong. Like for example yesterday I *could not find* the invoices I was supposed to file for Cindy—that's the Juniors buyer. I panicked for about fifteen minutes—it felt like *forever*—but then thank goodness I realized they were in the bathroom, on the counter. I should do nothing but find trends. Cindy just bought a shipment of paint-splattered raincoats because of me. I think they're gonna be huge!"

"That's great!" I grinned at her. I'd never cared about raincoat shipments in my life, but Merry made them feel important.

"But we can't just stand here in front of Juniors," she said then. "You've never been in the store before, right?"

I didn't answer—I felt confused and surprised. How exactly did she know that?

Without my even asking, she started ex-
plaining. "Gran—that's my grandmother—she's
worked for the city for decades; she knows
everything about everyone. Anyway, Gran says
your dad used to work here, then she said something about something—I'm not going to lie, I
tune her out sometimes, she talks and talks
and talks—but I'm pretty sure she said you'd
never been here, in your family's store, before.
Is that true?"

I nodded. "It's my first time."

"That's crazy." She shook her head at the cra-
ziness of it. "I'm going to show you everything."

"Great!" I said, and meant it. (The truth
is, I figured it'd be more fun seeing the store
with Merry than with you. Sorry—I know that's
mean. But you weren't exactly being your best
self at the time.)

Right then the glass doors opened behind
us. A man in a suit walked in, and I saw a few
other people outside, pulling out key cards.

"Hey, Bryce," Merry said.

Then she looked down at her watch, shook

her hands a little, and cried, "We have to go!"
She started speed-walking away from me down
the aisle, back very straight, arms pumping, feet
moving surprisingly quickly in her low-heeled
red sling-backs.

I hurried after her. "Where? Why?"

"Your grandmother told me to get you to the
dressing room by eight forty-five. We've got two
minutes!"

I tried looking all around as we passed department after department, but we were walking fast, and I couldn't take in much. We sped
by the cluster of mannequins wearing silky lavender nightgowns in Intimate Apparel. The tall
racks of pastel leather totes in Handbags, too.
And that table display of strappy heels in Ladies' Shoes.

We saw a few people setting up their departments. "Nicole!" Merry called to a red-headed
woman cleaning a glass case in Cosmetics.
When Nicole looked up, Merry pointed at me
and said, "Cat, the other granddaughter."

I waved and Nicole waved back. She didn't
seem surprised to see me—nobody did, that
whole day; everyone in the store seems to learn

news about your family at lightning speed—
but she was very interested. Definitely staring. I glanced back after we'd passed; she was
still looking. The woman locking a case in Fine
Jewelry waved at me, too, and did some staring
of her own. A man stepped out from between
racks of dresses in Ready-to-Wear, smiled as we
zoomed past, and said, "Welcome, Catarina!"

I blushed—it was bizarre, having all that attention. I didn't like it. I would've rather been
in Bloomingdale's or Saks, where the salespeople always ignored me entirely.

Then we turned into Designers, and I saw
you.

I'd thought it would just be you, waiting for me, watching from behind those glasses, ready to say something like, "We will also have to teach you how to comb your hair."

But of course you had other people with you—you were almost never alone in the store. I learned that quickly. You were always giving salespeople instructions or greeting customers or asking your assistant for something or meeting in a group with managers or buyers. I can only remember seeing you alone in one place: outside the door with the DO NOT ENTER sign on the second floor.

In Designers you stood with a crew around you, near the two mannequins wearing flouncy silk floral dresses. And you behaved really unexpectedly. For one thing, you didn't insult me. You introduced me politely instead. And you were so nice to those other people! "Salma is a consistent sales leader." "Richard is new to the store. I think he will be very good." "Ms. Diaz has been a trusted worker for many years." "Merry is always very stylish. We are lucky to have her with us this summer." (Merry got the biggest smile on her face when you said that.) You even made a joke, sort of. "We have Dara *and* Cara as department managers. It can be confusing!"

Everyone laughed, including Merry. They all truly seemed to like being around you. Obviously they could've been pretending, because you were the boss. But it didn't feel that way.

It was so weirdly different from how Aunt Miriam and Lexie seemed around you. They struggled—I could see it—figuring out how to deal with you. Even though they'd known you their whole lives.

These people were not struggling. They also paid way too much attention to me, once you'd finished the introductions. "Look somewhere else!" I wanted to tell them. They had all sorts of thoughts to share with me.

"We stayed after hours last night, pulling clothes for you," Cindy, the Juniors buyer, told me. "Ms. Gerta told us all about your dark hair and your pretty blue eyes. I think we got the right colors for you, and the right sizes."

I glanced over at you then. Had you really called my eyes pretty? I would've loved it if you had. But you just gazed back at me, unblinking. It made me furious with you again. All that niceness you were showing them—would it be so hard to save a tiny bit for me?

"It's funny, you living in New York and coming here to shop," Dara or Cara told me. "We always want to buy clothes there!"

"She doesn't like what I have," I said in a nasty tone, jutting my chin at you.

Nobody seemed to notice the nastiness. They laughed, and Salma said, "She has very high standards!"

A man who looked like Captain America in a business suit walked up to us then. He was carrying a tall stack of shoeboxes, each with a sticker that said 7.5—my size. I looked at you again. How had you known that, just looking down at my feet?

"In the middle dressing room please, Michael," you told the man. Then you said to me, "Come. I will show you a little more of the store before you try the clothes on."

I hoped you'd say something nice to me as we walked. Something like, "We are lucky to have you with us this summer, too, Catarina. I can see you have potential." But instead you focused entirely on the store. You led me up the escalator and showed me the Beauty Salon, with its black leather swivel chairs, tall oval mirrors, and jars filled with scissors and combs. "Rosa has cut my hair for years," you told me. "She is the best in the city."

You walked us through Travel, too, with its displays of toiletry kits, water bottles, and sleep masks. "We used to have a travel agency," you said, "until it stopped being profitable. In business it is important to adapt."

You took me to the Cafeteria and introduced me to Charlie and LuLu, who were scrambling eggs and making hash browns behind the counter. "You may eat your meals here on the days that you work," you told me. "Charlie and LuLu know to charge the food to my account."

You did not point out the door with the DO NOT ENTER sign near the Cafeteria and the Gift Wrap counter. Instead you rushed by it and said we needed to get back to Designers. But I saw it then for the first time, and I wondered what was back there. A safe, maybe? With jewels?

When we'd returned to Designers, you led me to the middle dressing room. It was ten times bigger than any fitting room I'd ever seen in New York. A three-way, full-length mirror took up much of the back wall, and rolling racks hanging with clothing lined the wall on the right. "These are not designer clothes," you told me. "You are not ready for that. But Designers has larger fitting rooms than Juniors, and we need the space."

"I'm only here for three weeks," I reminded you, looking at the rolling racks. "How many work outfits do I need?"

You ignored that. The Daras and the Caras all started streaming into the dressing room. "Cindy and I picked this one out together," Merry told me, holding up a cornflower-blue A-line dress. "We're rooting for it!"

Everyone looked at me expectantly, like the fate of the world depended on whether I liked cornflower-blue A-line.

"It's really pretty," I said.

Merry clapped a little, then clasped her hands in front of her and grinned at me. There was a weird silence after that. Everyone seemed to be waiting. A terrible thought hit me: *Am I*

supposed to start trying things on in front of them?
I remembered Lexie that morning saying something about dressing and undressing in front of
hordes of people. *Not going to happen, not in a
million years!* "If you wait out there," I told everybody, pointing out the door, "I'll try that one on
first."

"Of course!"

"Wonderful!"

"Can't wait to see it!"

Everyone filed out then, including you. One
older woman hung back, though. When it was
only the two of us, she took a step closer—she
smelled like baby powder—and said with a sad
look, "I worked with your father for many years.
I even remember when he was just five years
old and would go from department to department, picking up crumpled napkins and empty
drink cans. Please tell him Elisa Torres sends
her very best."

"I will," I promised. As she left I said her
name in my head a few times, *Elisa Torres, Elisa
Torres,* so I wouldn't forget.

After that I tried on the cornflower-blue
dress, which really was very pretty, and stepped

out to show everyone, and they all practically gave me a standing ovation. "Oh, you have to keep that one! It suits you so well—it's perfect with your eyes!" I'll admit it—it felt good, getting all that praise. But also ridiculous and embarrassing.

Fortunately after that almost everyone went back to work. You stayed in the Designers department, though, talking with employees and customers and commenting on my clothes whenever I came out. You said things I'd never heard before. I'm "long waisted" apparently, whatever that means—from the way you said it, I got that it's not ideal. I had a flash of feeling deformed, super stretched out between chest and hip. But then I told myself, *It's not like you have an arm growing out of your ear.* Plus I'd made it a lot of years without even knowing I had this problem, so how bad could it be? You also called some of the pants I tried on "too short in the crotch," which sounded gross. And you ordered one skirt sent back to the manufacturer because of mismatched seams. You even called the Juniors department and told the salesperson to check every one of the skirts in stock.

Apparently mismatched seams must be gotten rid of, like lice.

Eventually we found five outfits in flattering colors with acceptable necklines and waistlines and seams and crotches. We picked out shoes for each one, too. Then you made a call, and Inga from Alterations appeared with her tape measure and her doughnut-shaped pin cushion.

You told Inga exactly where to pin every piece of clothing. "The sides must come in." "The shoulders droop too low." "Take up the hem three-quarters of an inch." "The sleeves are a fraction too long."

You kept giving instructions, then walking out to do work, then returning. I got plenty tired, taking off clothes, putting on clothes, try-ing never to be too naked with people I barely knew. Holding very still while Inga pinned sides and shoulders and sleeves, then spinning slowly while she took up hems. I felt bad about how much stooping and standing she was doing—she looked about as old as you. But she was nimble and seemed quite used to it.

Still, I considered telling you it wasn't worth the time and effort. I'd never gone through all this bother with clothes before, and I'd survived fine. But it obviously mattered to you, a whole lot, so I kept quiet. Plus I could see you were right. Even with pins still in, everything was looking better with your changes.

We finally reached the last dress. "Hem it one-half inch, please," you told Inga. Then off you went.

I'd just turned a bit on the stand in front of the three-way mirror—Inga was about halfway through the hemming—when you burst back in.

"Give us a moment please, Inga," you said.

You looked so intense—you obviously wanted her to hustle out of there.

She did.

I felt like I should rush out after her and keep going far. Why'd you need to talk to me alone—what had I done? I couldn't think of anything, but there must be something—what was it?

Your eyes were on my face. "Your aunt Miriam is ready to call the police. Your cousin Lexie has disappeared."

I wanted to tell you the truth about Lexie. I hate lying—I'm terrible at it—plus I didn't want Uncle Bob grabbing one of his Revolutionary War rifles and going on a hunt for Lexie's kidnapper.

"No need to call anyone," I wanted to say. "She's safe and sound at the Piggly Wiggly."

But you would've asked why on earth Lexie had gone there, and I couldn't tell you that. She'd get in huge trouble for faking an illness so she could go meet her sketchy boyfriend— her parents already hated him—and I couldn't be the one to rat her out. I couldn't think of a single plausible lie for her being there, either. I couldn't actually say out loud any of the reasons that popped in my head. *She needed canned tuna.* Or, *She had a powerful craving for yogurts and cheeses.*

"They tried calling and texting her, right?" I finally said. Maybe she'd *just* seen or heard their messages. Maybe she was rushing home already, with the perfect excuse planned.

"Of course they have called and texted," you told me. "They say her phone is off. We—"

I tuned you out. Her phone must've died.

She probably had no idea she needed to get home *now*, before police officers started walking up and down the streets of her neighborhood with dogs, tracking her scent.

I guess you asked me a question while I was imagining those police dogs. I hadn't moved from the fitting-room stand, and I was still wearing a half-pinned lavender dress. When I focused back on you, you were watching and waiting.

"What?"

"I think you know something." You had one hand on your hip.

"I don't, I really don't." I made my eyes super wide and felt my face turn pink and moist. One of the pins from Inga's half hem was scratching above my knee, but I couldn't move my leg away from it. I felt weirdly frozen.

You laughed a little and shook your head. "You're an even worse liar than your father when he was your age."

I was so glad you gave me that change of topic!

"Did he lie to you a lot back then?" I asked

quickly. "What kind of lies? About friends or homework or grades? Did he lie about his grades?"

You didn't answer. You just looked at me steadily from behind your glasses. I kept going.

"How'd you know when he was lying? Did he get all flushed and sweaty like me? I like hearing ways we're similar. I don't know anything about him when he was a boy."

Still no answer. Which was risky on your part! I could've gotten all huffy about how you were the reason I didn't know anything about his past. I didn't, though. Not at that point. I plowed ahead.

"Did you punish him? How? Was it just time-outs or worse?" What would be worse than time-outs? I actually got a little worked up, imagining that.

You'd crossed your arms by that point, and you were looking at me like I was a toddler jumping up and down on my bed when I was supposed to be going to sleep.

"Stop talking, and listen," you said. It was rude, but effective. I listened. "I am guessing

Lexie had a plan to sneak out, a plan that you know about. Right?"

I pretended I was you and didn't even consider answering.

"So you think she is safe," you continued, "but you don't really know. What if something went wrong with this plan? Lexie takes risks—she is often not smart in the way she behaves. And young people are unwise. You don't yet know danger. You must tell me where she is."

I crossed my arms too then and raised my chin. You made the whole not-ratting-Lexie-out thing so easy for me. *Maybe* if you'd been nice, *maybe* you could've gotten me to say something. But calling Lexie stupid, and me and Lexie both unwise, and telling me what I did and didn't know—that was *not* the right move.

"You have no idea whether I know danger." I felt weirdly large right then, and rock-solid. "I only met you *yesterday*. You're supposed to be family, but you've never visited me, never once called me on the phone, never even sent me a birthday card. You're wrong about me. You don't know a thing."

(I do understand that I'm a very lucky person, and billions of people live in way worse situations than me. But I can still know danger. I once saw a rat the size of a beagle scurrying along a subway platform, heading right for me.)

If you were bothered by my whole "you don't write, you don't call; don't pretend you know me" speech, you didn't show it. You didn't try to defend your rotten past behavior, either. Instead you said something monumentally stupid.

"If you do not tell me where Lexie is, I won't buy you those pretty clothes."

My face turned into a hot iron then, I was so angry. I started unzipping the half-hemmed dress, ready to take it off in front of you, that's how mad you'd made me.

"I don't want these clothes!" I had one arm wrapped behind me, struggling to unzip that thing. "I'm only trying them on because you hate my other clothes—which I *like*! I don't have to work here; I don't have to dress the way you want me to; I'm *fine*."

You held up a hand to stop me; I'd finally gotten the zipper to the middle of my back.

"I want you to have the clothes," you said. "And I want you to work here."

"You do?"

It was the only nice thing you'd ever said to me. I stood there for a second, dress gaping at the top, letting it register. Then I got annoyed *again*—*that* was the only way you were going to be nice? Giving me the honor of *working* for you?

"We're wasting time," you told me then. "Someone could have taken Lexie, they could have discarded or destroyed her phone. The longer we wait, the harder it might be to find her."

It was a possibility. I decided right then I had to get rid of you, get out of the store, and go check the Piggly Wiggly. As far as I knew I couldn't walk there; I needed someone to drive me. Someone who wasn't you. Someone I wouldn't have to pay, since I'd left my wallet at Lexie's.

"I might be able to fix this," I told you. "But I need you to leave me alone. And I need Merry."

Merry hustled across the parking lot toward her car. "This is an adventure! The office phone never rings for me, who would call me there? My friends know to text me during work and I'll get back to them when I can. When the phone rang and Cindy said, 'Hi, Ms. Gerta,' I was already surprised, because Ms. Gerta always stops by the office on her rounds, she almost never calls. *Then* Cindy said, 'Sure, one second,' and handed the phone to *me*! I almost dropped it. It's not like Ms. Gerta doesn't know who I am—she knows everybody. But why would she call me? I thought maybe I was being fired. But then she just said, 'I need you to take Catarina on an errand.'"

She'd stopped at the smallest—and brightest green—car I'd ever seen.

She laughed at the way I was looking at it.

"It's like a car for leprechauns, right? I love it. But my friends call it the Great Green Pea. Climb in!"

I was squished inside that car, and I'm not nearly as long as Merry. Once she'd folded herself into the driver's seat, she was all elbows and knees.

"Where to?" she asked, glancing at me over a bent elbow.

"The Piggly Wiggly," I said. "And fast—as fast as we can go without getting in an accident or pulled over by the cops."

"Okay!" she said. "But what kind of crisis could there possibly be at the Piggly Wiggly? And which one are we going to?"

"There's more than one?"

She nodded. "There're one in Clarice's old neighborhood, and one out by Aunt Stella. I drove past one way far out just the other day. Where was I? On Choctaw, I think. And then there's one under the overpass. No, that's wrong—that's Bct-R—Mom loves their deli counter."

I couldn't believe it. How many Piggly Wigglys could a town possibly need? "I want the one you could walk to from Azalea Street." I thought for a second, remembering the street sign on Lexie's corner. "And St. Rose."

She backed the Great Green Pea up. "The one on Government's a couple of miles from there, but it's closest." We zipped across the lot. "Want to tell me what's going on?"

"Hang on a second." I was texting and calling Lexie. The voicemail kept picking right up, the way it does when there's no chance of the person answering. It got me a little worried. What if someone *had* grabbed her and thrown her phone into a swamp?

I got the number for the Piggly Wiggly on Government while Merry pressed on the gas and zoomed us through a yellow light.

Someone picked up after a few rings. "Piggly Wiggly. Jarrod speaking."

"Um—" I wasn't sure what exactly to say. "I need to speak to Hank?"

"Riiight, Haannk," Jarrod said. Weirdly knowingly.

"Who's Hank?" Merry said, scooting around a slow-moving pickup. "How do you know a Hank?"

I shook my head at her.

"Who's calling please?" Jarrod was saying, in a teasing tone. "Let's take this alphabetically. Is it Ally? Betsy? Deb? Helen? Faye?"

I didn't like that. Why would so many girls be calling Hank? Besides—

"F comes before H," I told Jarrod.

"Huh?"

"Faye, then Helen. Alphabetically."

I hung up. I couldn't depend on mocking, idiotic Jarrod for help. And I didn't want him knowing our business.

Luckily, Merry was already turning into the Piggly Wiggly lot.

"What're we looking for?" she asked, unbuckling her seat belt and throwing open her door.

I thought about saying "ground beef" and sending her off to find that, keeping Lexie's secret a little longer. But Merry was going to have to drive Lexie home if all went well, or help me find her somewhere else if it didn't. So I said, "Lexie. We're looking for Lexie. She should be with her boyfriend, Hank. He works here. We're keeping all that secret, though. Our grandmother doesn't know. Okay?"

"Got it. I hear you." She pretended to lock her mouth and throw away the key. "I'm glad it's not you, though. Sneaking off to the grocery store to hang out with your boyfriend, Hank. I've been there—for me it was Jackson at the community theater. I was Rizzo in *Grease*. He worked on sets." She shook her head, still all folded up in the driver's seat of the car. "Jackson."

"Can we go?"

"Yes, of course, let's go!"

We climbed out of the Great Green Pea and hurried into the supermarket.

"We're looking for a Hank," she said in a very professional voice to a woman bagging groceries. "We understand he works here."

"Just saw him heading in the direction of Fresh Meats," the woman said, pointing down an aisle toward a counter at the back.

I rushed that way while behind me Merry said, "Thanks. Tell me, how well do you know Hank?"

It was cold in Fresh Meats. I saw raw chicken packages on lit shelves, plus marbled steaks. The only person in sight was a wide, bald man wearing a bloodied white apron. I assumed it wasn't Hank—he was wide and bald and old! But what did I actually know? I was about to say, "Hank?" when someone said, "Cat?" I turned—it was Lexie, calling to me from Bulk Foods.

"Where's your phone?!" I hissed at her, hurrying over.

"Dead," she said. "I forgot to charge it." She pointed to one of the tubes of bulk food. "Want a handful of trail mix? It's delicious! Don't worry about paying. They don't care at all, as long as they don't see you."

I grabbed her by the arm and started pulling her out of the store. "You have to get home *right now*."

You have to hand it to Lexie. She has her flaws, but when the pressure is on, she can think fast. Before she'd even squished herself into the back seat of the leprechaun car, she'd started telling me and Merry what we had to do to help her out of the mess she'd made. If we'd had pen and paper, she probably would've drawn charts.

"Don't drive us all the way to the house," she told Merry, as we pulled out of our Piggly Wiggly parking spot. (It felt like Lexie was in the middle of the front seat, even though she was in the back, that's how small the Great Green Pea is.) "Stop a block before and let us out."

"I guess one block's okay," Merry said. "But Ms. Gerta would want me to bring you home, and I don't want to lose my job. So you can't go messing around."

"Got it," Lexie said. Then, as we drove along, she laid out her grand vision. The basic idea was: After Merry dropped us off, I would walk sadly to the front door of the house, ring the doorbell, look all dejected, and say I hadn't found Lexie. This would give Lexie time to sneak back up her tree, climb through her window, then pretend she'd fainted in the Duck Room. As soon as someone went in there, she'd groggily wake up and say she'd gotten so disoriented in her debilitating sickness, she'd thought she was actually in her room. That was the last thing she remembered—thinking she was in her room. Then she'd gone out like a light.

"Mom and Dad will feel so bad when they see me in my catatonic state, they'll pamper me until I say I'm better. It's the perfect plan."

Lexie looked super satisfied with herself. I had a lot of questions, though. Would I be able to lie well enough, or would everyone know instantly that I actually had found Lexie? What if someone had closed and locked Lexie's window by now—did she have a plan B? What about the biscuits that Rose-Marie had given Lexie to bring upstairs—what'd happened to them?

I started with that last thought. "Wouldn't you have been holding that plate of Rose-Marie's biscuits when you got all disoriented?"

"You're right!" Lexie looked at me with new respect, like she was realizing I might actually be useful for future schemings. "Where did I put the biskwi?"

"We have other problems!" Merry was

slowing the car down and pointing out the wind-shield.

There, running straight down the middle of the street, waving both arms at us, was Aunt Miriam, in her business blouse and pencil skirt and expensive heels.

"I didn't know she could run," Lexie said.

Then she slumped over, suddenly too sick to sit up.

Aunt Miriam was already at Merry's window, knocking on it, motioning for Merry to roll it down.

"Here goes," Merry said shakily, pressing the button for the window.

In an instant Aunt Miriam was leaning in, glaring at Lexie. I was glad she wasn't looking for me. Her face wasn't just red from running—she was *livid*.

"Alexandra Rosenfeldt!" she hissed.

It took me a second to understand—I'd forgotten Lexie was short for Alexandra.

"I might be an idiot once in a day," Aunt Miriam spat out, still leaning in and scowling at Lexie, "but not twice! You're healthy as a horse.

Get out of that car right now. You could not be more grounded."

I started scrambling out of the car fast, because it was a two-door and Lexie couldn't get out until I'd folded my seat forward. Which took a painful few seconds—I had trouble finding the right lever.

Meanwhile Aunt Miriam turned to Merry, who was leaning away from her, giving her space. "My mother called to tell me to be on the lookout for your car." Aunt Miriam's voice was much nicer now. "Thank you for going to get Lexie. Where'd you find her?"

"Um . . ." Merry looked a little guiltily at me, which was very kind of her. She was obviously remembering that she'd promised to keep our trip a secret. I shrugged and gave her a *don't worry about it* look. I didn't want her risking her job, especially since Lexie was doomed regardless.

"The Piggly Wiggly on Government," Merry told Aunt Miriam.

"The Piggly Wiggly on Government," Aunt Miriam repeated slowly, her eyes shooting daggers at Lexie as she climbed out of the car.

Once Lexie was fully out, Aunt Miriam said, "To the house." She looked ready to pull Lexie there by her hair, but Lexie started meekly walking on her own. Aunt Miriam followed right behind her.

I kept standing by the car, not sure what to do. Aunt Miriam hadn't told me goodbye—was she expecting me to go with them? I hoped not. I didn't want to get caught in that battle. Plus I wasn't sure how Aunt Miriam was feeling about me. She must've figured out that I'd known to look for Lexie at the Piggly Wiggly. Did she think I'd supported Lexie's plan for lying and sneaking out? Maybe egged her on?

Part of me wanted to say, *I had nothing to do with this.* But a bigger part couldn't do that to Lexie.

"I'm going back to the store with Merry," I called after them instead.

Aunt Miriam turned and looked surprised, like she'd either forgotten about me or assumed I was with them.

"No," she said. "That's not the plan. You're

coming back to the house with us." She didn't sound angry. Just indifferent.

I had a flash of remembering how nice she'd been about my mom's spinach.

She'd never before seemed like she didn't care about me one way or the other. I hated that feeling. It definitely would've felt better if she'd yelled at me. Then at least I could've told myself she was being unfair. And I wouldn't have felt like a stranger who didn't matter.

"Safta can't look out for you in the store right now," Aunt Miriam told me, in the same, flat voice. "She has too much going on. And she's leaving a little early, to make Shabbat dinner for you."

She looked at Lexie then, and her face turned plenty angry. "Not you. You're not leaving home again for a very long time."

Uncle Bob met us at the front door. I'm used to him being a jolly, booming, "How-Is-Everyone-Today?" kind of person. Not in that moment, though. In that moment, in the silver-and-white foyer that looks like it's gift wrapped for Christmas, he was quiet and serious and laser focused on Lexie. As he stepped aside to let us in, he asked her in the lowest—and scariest—voice I'd ever heard him use, "Not so sick after all, were you?"

Then he and Aunt Miriam both went into attack mode, firing questions at Lexie, talking over each other, not even giving her a chance to answer:

"What do we have to do to make you *listen*?"

"After all that we've done for you, all that we've given you, *this* is how you thank us?"

"If it were the first time, it would be one thing. What's that saying again?"

"First time, shame on you. Second time, shame on us. Do you see why we're thinking of that particular saying, Lexie?"

"What are we going to do to make sure there's no next time? What should we do? If you were us, what would *you* do?"

I kept my eyes on the ground and started moving slowly away as they talked on and on. I had to get out of there. I didn't want Lexie thinking I liked watching her get yelled at.

I was only a few steps from the living room, mere moments from freedom, when Aunt Miriam said, "Cat."

I stopped midstep, then turned back slowly, biting my lower lip and waiting for Aunt Miriam to say things like, "How long exactly did you know Lexie was at the Piggly Wiggly? Why didn't you tell us sooner? You could've saved us a lot of worry!"

Instead, Aunt Miriam said, in a very serious voice, "I will talk to you later. Go on upstairs."

I didn't want to talk to her later, but I was perfectly happy not to talk to her then. I rushed off to our room.

I found Rose-Marie's biskwi piled on a plate on Lexie's dresser. Thank goodness, too. I was hungry! It'd been a long time since breakfast. I walked straight to the plate and started eating.

Obviously my biscuit would've been better right out of the oven, soft and warm, with melting butter. But it was still plenty delicious. I was licking my fingers when I heard the sound of raised voices. I quickly grabbed my book and my phone and went to hide in the leopard-skin library. Not a moment too soon, either. I'd just slid down low on the couch when Aunt Miriam and Lexie both stormed down the hall.

"No electronics for three weeks," Aunt Miriam was saying angrily. "No phone, no laptop, no calculator. No Bayou Country Music Jam, either. You are staying *home*."

I thought for sure Lexie would get worked up about the Bayou Country Music Jam—she'd been so excited about seeing that Slick Billy group. Instead she said, very sarcastically, "I don't know *what* I'll do without a calculator."

They must've turned the corner then. As their voices faded, my phone dinged with a text from Max.

Hola. Que pasa in Baton Rouge?

I wrote right back.

Lexie in huge Hank trouble! No electronics for her for three weeks.

None at all? No AC, no microwave? No
water pick?

What's a water pick?

That wand thing that shoots water at your
teeth. Like flossing, but easier on the gums.

No one uses water picks.

Those of us with good dental
hygiene do.

I have good dental hygiene!

He didn't respond right away.
I started running my tongue along my teeth,
worrying about my dental hygiene for the first
time ever.
Finally he started typing again.

Mom annoyed bc I'm texting during dessert.

She's right! Give dessert your full
attention!

Adios then.

Adios.

I set my phone on the couch beside me and started wondering what dessert Max was eating. I suddenly wanted dessert myself, which reminded me: I was supposed to go to Shabbat dinner at your house.

Then I started dreading that dinner. For lots of reasons. I'd had a rotten time the only other time I'd been at your house, for the fried chicken lunch. And I hated the idea of doing something Jewish with you. I figured it'd be a big Judaism Test for Cat, and I'd definitely fail.

I wasn't a complete Shabbat idiot—I'd been to a couple of Shabbat dinners at my friend Rachel's house before she moved to Dallas in fifth grade. I knew people said blessings over candles and challah and other things. But I had no idea what the blessings actually were. I knew you'd judge me for not knowing. And I knew you'd blame Mom—wrongly! I didn't want to hear it. I definitely considered refusing to go.

I tried reading for a while, to distract myself,

but it didn't ease my sense of dread. Still, when Rose-Marie found me in the library and told me, "Time to go see your granmær," I got up right away. I didn't want to seem bratty to Rose-Marie, who knew my dad long ago and was always so nice to me and made delicious biskwi. I wanted her to like me.

So I headed off to your house without complaining. But that doesn't mean I was happy.

We'd had one of those late-afternoon Louisiana thundershowers while I was in the leopard-skin library, and rays of light streamed through dark clouds as I crossed the street. I was still wearing the coral dress I'd had on all day; by that point it was very wrinkled. As I walked past your Cadillac and knocked on your back door, I got ready for you to attack my clothes the way you had the last time I'd stood in that spot—I was even considering saying, "Your *face* is wrinkled," as a comeback. That's how defensive I was feeling.

But you didn't say a single word when you opened the door. You just stepped aside for me to come in.

Right away I noticed something weird: muddy paw prints on your otherwise spotless kitchen floor. Then I heard the yap of the little yellow dog sitting in the kitchen, wagging its tail, its eyes only on you.

"You got a dog?"

I couldn't believe it. I hadn't known you long, but you did *not* seem like someone who would want an animal getting dirty prints and hairs on your floor and clothes. Plus you worked all the time. You couldn't just leave this dog alone all day every day—that'd be cruel!

"It's not mine," you told me. Good thing, too, because I was getting pretty worked up on that dog's behalf.

It clearly loved you, though. Its tail *thwap-thwap-thwap*ped against the black-and-white tile floor as you moved to the stove and started stirring something in a small pot. I wondered what you were making us for our Shabbat dinner—it smelled really good. But, turned out, it wasn't for us.

"Your soup is almost ready," you told the dog. "Lentil, your favorite. Be patient."

I don't have a dog, but I've visited plenty of people who do. And I've never once heard any of them say, "Come, Fido. Let's heat you up some soup." But you stirred for a while, then poured every last drop out of the pot into a metal bowl and set it on the floor for the dog, who started lapping it right up.

I got a little offended at that point. Was *I* getting any soup? Was it dinner for the dog and nothing but prayers for me?

"His name is Oscar," you said, smiling at the

dog. He glanced up when you said his name, but only for a second. He quickly went back to eating his soup. "He belongs to my neighbors. But he loves coming here."

You were looking at that dog with way more affection than you'd ever looked at anyone, as far as I'd seen. I looked at him, too, and thought, *What's your secret, Oscar?* He was licking the bowl clean now.

"He's not the cutest dog," you whispered, like you didn't want him to hear you insult him. It was true—his body was too wide for his head. Probably because you kept feeding him soup. "But he is very smart," you said more loudly. "I was never very cute, either. But I have always been smart."

It hit me then, when you said "I have always been smart"—something I'd known all along, obviously, but never really thought through: At some point you were a girl, like me. You'd known you were smart. How? Did you know all the answers in class? Did you get As? Did they give As in Germany?

I wanted to ask, "What were you like as a

kid?" But that felt too weird. Instead I said, "Did you have a dog when you were a girl?"

You didn't answer. Your face went completely blank, like someone had flipped a switch to turn it off. You took a step away from me and grabbed Oscar's bowl and started scrubbing it in the sink, hard.

I knew I'd said the wrong thing—I felt like I'd failed the simplest "Talking to Safta" test— but how? I'd only asked whether you had a dog. I hated that feeling: obviously doing something wrong, but at the same time, as far as I could tell, doing nothing wrong at all.

Oscar walked over to you as you scrubbed, and started butting your leg with his head.

You turned off the water then and smiled down at him. It was good to see you smiling again. "That's how he tells me he wants more," you told me. "He hits me with his head."

You dried your hands on a dish towel and told him, "You know you can't have more. Your parents will get angry with me."

Then you walked to the back door and opened it for him. "Out you go."

He gave you one goodbye yap and stepped out the door, his wide belly swaying.

"He'll be back tomorrow," you told me, shutting the door behind him. "Now come. We will say our prayers."

I didn't like those words—"our prayers"—it sounded like you were assuming I knew the Shabbat prayers, when I didn't. Plus I was already feeling like I didn't understand how to behave, and I was weirdly jealous of Oscar the Dog, who got you smiling in a way I definitely couldn't.

So once I'd followed you through the swinging door into the same dining room where you'd insulted my mom's spinach, and I saw the tall white candles standing in the silver candlesticks near your place at the table, and the silver kiddush cup, and the white embroidered cloth covering the plate with challah, and the tattered prayer book, I went on a little rant.

"I don't know the prayers, okay?" I told you. "And it's not my mom's fault, so don't even think that. My mom *wants* us to do Shabbat. She likes buying challah from this bakery in our neighborhood, a couple of times she even set stuff out, like you did"—I waved in the direction of the candles—"and she asked Dad to read the prayers. But *he* wouldn't do it. He's the one who thinks organized religion ruins families."

I stopped myself from saying, "And *you're* the reason he thinks that. It's *your* fault." It felt too mean to say. But the message must've been clear.

You didn't have much visible reaction to my rant. You stood there, blinking at me and looking a little pale. Then you said, in a very straightforward tone, "Your father has made his own decisions for a long time. You are old enough to make yours. Would you like to make Shabbat with me?"

That tone made it very hard to stay angry with you. I couldn't even fully remember what you'd done to make me so rant-y. Fed a dog soup? Said "our prayers"?

I wasn't going to turn and walk out on you. Plus I love the taste of challah.

So I said, "Yes. I'd like to make Shabbat with you."

You smiled at me then, just as nicely as you'd smiled at Oscar the Dog.

"I would let you use my prayer book," you told me, "but it is in Hebrew and German. No English. It doesn't matter—I know the prayers by heart. I will teach you. I set out the prayer book because I like the feel of it. I like to hold it."

It was the most you'd ever told me about yourself. You knew the prayers by heart. You liked the feel of the tattered prayer book; you liked to hold it. I had the weirdest sensation, as if I was taking those little pieces of information and folding them up and placing them in a shirt pocket over my heart.

The room had grown dark—the sun, which had broken through the clouds after the storm, was now setting outside. With a flare of light you lit a long match, then each of the two candles.

"We wave our hands three times above the candles now, to welcome Shabbat," you said, showing me how. "Then we cover our eyes and say the blessing." Slowly you taught me the prayer: *"Baruch atah Adonai, Eloheinu Melech ha'olam . . ."*

You waited for me to say each word until I got it right. Remember how much trouble I had with the "ch" sound? "Clear your throat as you say it," you told me. "Like you have a piece of carrot stuck there. *Ch. Ch. Ch.*"

It took a long time for us to get through the whole prayer, then the ones for the wine and the challah. But you didn't seem to mind. And I liked learning something that meant so much to you. I didn't feel guilty about Mom, either. I need to tell you this over and over, so you'll really believe it: She's always wanted me to be more connected to Judaism. And to you.

After we'd finished the prayer over the bread, we tore off pieces of your homemade challah, golden brown on the outside and perfectly braided. Then we had the dinner you'd made for us. (Of course you hadn't only cooked for Oscar.) It had all been in the oven: brisket with roast potatoes and green beans. No spinach. Everything was going so well—the food so delicious, the lit candles so pretty, no mean words said—until I asked what turned out to be a terrible question.

"Where did you get that kiddush cup?" I asked. "It's beautiful."

It was just something to say, really. The cup was sitting in front of me; it looked antique and had swirly etchings; in spots it reflected the flickering of the candles.

But you stopped eating—you set your fork down and looked off in the distance, and I noticed your hand shaking. You seemed so weak, so suddenly frail, I got ready to stand up fast and catch you if you fell off your chair. *What should I do?* I thought. *What should I do?*

I didn't remember that the notepad in your hall had the name of a doctor written on it, along with a phone number. I wish I had.

Just as I was wondering whether I should call Aunt Miriam, you seemed better. You looked at me and raised your chin and said, "What? You don't like my food? You're not eating."

I was so relieved to hear you sounding okay, I didn't ask any questions. I started eating too fast and didn't even mind much when you said,

"I see I have to teach you manners, too. Cut smaller pieces and chew, chew, chew."

I should've asked questions, though. To this day I don't know: Were you shaken because of sickness that night? Or were you remembering your father in Germany handing you the kiddush cup as he said goodbye?

It wasn't particularly late when we finished dinner, including your butter cookies for dessert, and I only had to walk back across the street, and the streetlamps were lit. Still, you called Aunt Miriam to let her know I was on my way, plus you switched on your front door light for me and stood out there on the stoop, waiting. I could feel you watching the whole way as I headed out under the dark denim sky. Once I'd reached the house and Aunt Miriam had opened their door for me, I turned and waved. Only then did the light on your front stoop go out.

I liked the feeling of knowing that you cared whether I made it those fifty feet. It wrapped me up, like a comfy sweater. But it vanished the second Aunt Miriam started talking.

"I've been wanting to speak with you, Cat," she said. "Come in the living room and have a seat."

I wanted to say, *No thanks!* and duck under her arm and sprint upstairs. But I stayed put. Because I'm not six.

Lexie did something wrong, not me, I kept

reminding myself as Aunt Miriam ushered me into their fancy living room with its enormous Oriental rug. She took a seat in the middle of her firm sofa, beneath the painting of the moonlit marsh, and pointed me to a chair with a high back and carved wooden arms. I sat at the edge of that stiff chair and gripped my hands in my lap and tried to stop my heart from beating so fast. I don't like when grown-ups are disappointed in me. And I didn't know what was about to happen—would Aunt Miriam take away my electronics, too?

I actually thought, *Good thing I don't have a water pick*, and had to stop myself from nervous laughter.

Aunt Miriam was taking some time straightening little pillows on her right. Sitting there, watching her, I wanted to shake my hands and say, *Let's get this over with!* But one thing I was starting to realize about Aunt Miriam: She likes things perfect in her house. Throw pillows, coffee-table books, decorative dishes—she enjoys straightening them.

When she finished with the pillows, she

leaned toward me with a frown line between her eyebrows.

"Uncle Bob and I want to apologize for how your visit is going."

She might as well have said, "I was born with an extra nose." That's how surprising her apology was.

I stared at her.

"We're sorry about how it's going," she said, louder and slower. Like maybe I'd lost some hearing. "We don't want you to have a bad time."

"I'm not," I told her. One hundred percent truthfully. I was having a strange time. It wasn't exactly fun. But it wasn't *bad*.

"I'm glad to hear that." She looked like she didn't believe me. "Listen." She pointed one thin, manicured finger at me. "Don't get what I'm about to say wrong. Uncle Bob and I have talked about this, and we want you to stay. We really do."

I blinked at her. They'd talked about it? Sat together and debated it? *"Do we want Cat to stay? Would it be better if she left?"*

That hurt my feelings.

Aunt Miriam kept going.

"We know Lexie's behavior is making it harder for you to enjoy your visit. She'll be punished now for the rest of your time here. We don't want you to feel stuck. We just want you to know, we understand if you choose to go. We'll set it up with your parents."

She was making some sense, actually. Lexie might be hugely cranky for the rest of my stay. She might not want me around, just watching her be in trouble. Maybe I should go.

I looked away from Aunt Miriam and out a window onto the street I'd just crossed, with you watching. I remembered the glow of the light from the candles and repeating each word of the prayers with you. I remembered little Oscar, and that one second when you smiled at me the way you'd smiled at him. I decided then. I liked having a connection with you, or at least the start of one. I wanted to know whether you'd brought your tattered prayer book, which you liked to hold, with you when you left Germany. I guessed there was something you weren't saying about having a dog when you were a girl, and maybe something about your kiddush cup; I wanted to understand.

Besides, I had nothing to do back in New York. I'd canceled my camps and lost Blondie and Glitter, my two rotten friends. And Max would be in Greece until July.

"I want to stay," I told Aunt Miriam.

"Good," she said, her frown line fading. Which was a relief. What if it had deepened?

As I followed her out of the room she stopped at a side table to turn a bowl about an eighth of an inch. "Oh!" she said, when she'd finished. "I forgot to mention—your new clothes were delivered. We put them on your bed for you."

"Thanks," I told her. I hadn't realized clothes could be altered and delivered so fast. Turns out they can, when your grandmother owns the store and wants them to be.

I went upstairs and found on my bed two large white boxes with "Gerta's-Gerta's-Gerta's" written over and over in pretty blue script. My new pants and shirts were all neatly folded inside and wrapped in the same color blue tissue paper. There were Gerta's-Gerta's-Gerta's hanging bags, too, protecting my new dresses. It felt a little magical to have all those new clothes appear—clothes that had been picked out especially for me. I was tempted to lay every single piece on the bed and look at them all for a while, maybe put some on.

But I didn't want anyone walking in on me doing that. So I set the hanging bags on a doorknob and the boxes on the floor, out of the way. Then I sat on my bed and took my phone from my pocket, to call my parents.

Except, before I dialed, I started to wonder what I could possibly say about my day. Everything was tricky. They didn't know you'd bought me a million clothes—what if they didn't like that? What if they insisted on paying and there was an argument? We didn't need more arguments.

Our Shabbat dinner could be a problem, too. Dad would probably hate my doing something Jewish with you—he might assume you were trying to pull me away from Mom.

And then there was the whole Lexie-running-off-to-be-with-her-forbidden-boyfriend disaster. What would they say about that?

I was still sitting on my bed, not calling home and not texting Max, either, since it was the middle of the night in Greece, when Lexie wandered back into the room, drying her hands on her shorts.

"Good, you're finally back," she said, sitting beside me. "You've been gone forever—give me your phone."

"Why?"

"Mom took mine. And we need to text Hank."

"No, we definitely don't."

I did *not* like what that other Piggly Wiggly boy had said about Hank. Plus Lexie didn't need to be contacting him; she was in enough trouble already.

I should've been holding my phone tighter—Lexie reached over and grabbed it.

She held it high and started texting. I tried taking it back, but she leaned away from me and kept texting, completely ignoring me as I crawled over her and tried to get it.

Finally she pressed send and smiled at me, and handed it back.

I couldn't believe the text she'd written.

It's Lex. Parents took phone. This is
nerdy cousin's. Meet me tomorrow
morning at Safta's store.

"You can't meet him tomorrow at the store!"
I told her. "You're under house arrest!"
She grinned at me. "Watch and see."

I tried talking Lexie out of it. I told her being stuck at home without electronics for three weeks was bad enough—what would her parents do if she got caught lying *again*, to be with stupid Hank, who they hated? "They might send you to boarding school—then you'd *never* see him," I told her.

Lexie waved all that away and stayed very focused on my phone. After Hank had texted back (Cool, he texted. That's it. Just Cool), she happily got ready for bed and fell sound asleep. I got in bed, too, and started thinking of walking through your store, looking all around, saying hello to people here and there, until I drifted off.

The next morning I put on the navy dress you bought for me, with the white bands at the bottom of each sleeve and the top of each pocket. The dress hit just above my knee, which felt too long. Also I felt kind of like I should be wearing white gloves and pulling back my hair into a neat bun at my neck, and speaking with a lilt in my voice. I didn't feel like myself, is the point I'm trying to make. But still. I did look nice. I understand why you liked it.

I found something in the boxes besides clothes, too—an employee name tag, with CATA-RINA printed in blue. You must've had it made for me. I pinned it on in what I hoped was the right spot, looking down, double-checking that it was straight. It made me feel good, like you'd given me an award.

When Lexie finished dressing, she looked ridiculously like an angel. White blouse with a ruffle at the bottom of each puffed, short sleeve; white pants; white sandals; hair smoothed and tucked behind each ear; face very respectful.

"They're not going to forget you're punished just because you're wearing white," I told her.

"I understand why everyone is upset with the way I've behaved," she said, keeping her deeply deferential look. Obviously trying out her penitent daughter routine.

I rolled my eyes. "Let's just go."

In the kitchen Uncle Bob gave us a hearty "Don't you both look nice!" Aunt Miriam was reading some report, not paying much attention. But when Rose-Marie leaned over Lexie to set a plate of Belgian waffles on the table, I heard her mutter, "What are you up to, ti fiy?"

Lexie kept her eyes on Uncle Bob and her face very obedient.

"Daddy," she said. "I've been thinking."

That was the first time I'd ever heard her call Uncle Bob "Daddy." It'd always been "Dad" before.

Don't fall for it! I thought, trying to send him brain waves. I didn't want to spend my whole morning worrying about whether Lexie was sneaking off with scuzzy Hank. Plus what if you were actually sick? You didn't need the extra burden of a lying, sneaking Lexie.

Uncle Bob and Aunt Miriam were both focused on Lexie now. And to give them credit, they did both seem skeptical about her angel act. At first, anyway.

"I'm sorry for what I did," she told them, hands folded on the table by her plate, face still full of respect for all humankind. "I never should've lied. And I understand why you want me to stay home with no electronics. I know you have my best interests at heart, I truly do."

"I should hope so," Uncle Bob said, nodding with gusto and reaching over with his fork to spear the top Belgian waffle.

"I'm just wondering," Lexie continued, "whether instead of sitting here doing nothing—"

"You have no one to blame for that but yourself." Aunt Miriam's frown line was deeper than ever.

Stand strong! I beamed that message to Aunt Miriam with my eyes and mind.

Lexie actually put her hand over her heart. "I *do* blame myself. I do. But, as a punishment, maybe it'd be better if I did something *productive*. Like go work at Safta's store. You know I don't like working there—it's not like I want to be there. But maybe having that responsibility would be better for me."

Noooo! I thought, in a silent scream, after that little speech. Because Aunt Miriam and Uncle Bob were now looking questioningly at each other.

"I just think," Lexie continued, speaking so very reasonably, "if I'm occupied, I won't be sitting here wondering how to get around the rules. I'll be helping customers, learning business, developing a stronger relationship with Safta. Wouldn't that be better?"

Aunt Miriam was tapping one of her scary

manicured fingers on the table and pressing her lips together, thinking.

Hank is going to the store. I stared hard at her, trying to send her that message. *He will be at the store.*

Turns out, she's terrible at receiving brain waves. After another glance at Uncle Bob, she said, "It's true that no one will be able to keep much of an eye on you at home. We're meeting the deer blind sales rep at the hunting store this morning, and Rose-Marie will have her hands full here." (I assumed deer blinds were window treatments decorated with deer. I learned later they're hiding places from which to kill deer. Sometimes I wish I could stay ignorant about my family.)

Uncle Bob actually nodded.

"Don't geaux to ammo and camo!" I wanted to shout at both of them. "Stay home! Guard your lying child!"

Lexie kept making her case. "Safta will watch me like a hawk. Plus she has a whole staff to help."

Aunt Miriam and Uncle Bob nodded to each other.

"I'll check with Safta and make sure that works for her." Aunt Miriam set her napkin on the table and stood. "If she says yes, Lexie, you must promise to do everything she tells you."

"I swear." Lexie raised one hand like she was in court.

Uncle Bob said something about it being nice to see her take responsibility. I wasn't really listening. I was watching Rose-Marie, and we were both shaking our heads.

Aunt Miriam dropped me and Lexie at the store that morning and told us to go find you in Ladies' Shoes. We ran into Merry first. She was hustling up the aisle in front of Hats, looking perfect in a sleeveless blouse with a flowy wrap skirt and hoop earrings. She paused for a second to point at me and said, "Love the dress!" I grinned, but before I could thank her, she said, "Gotta run— sorry—I have to approve a shipment of denim shorts before we open." And she was off.

Lexie and I walked together through Cosmetics. Everything looked so pretty and clean there, with light bouncing off the glass-front cases and the silver-framed mirrors. All of the makeup was arranged so neatly, too: blushes and powders lined up from dark shades to light, perfumes in see-through bottles, rainbows of eye shadows. I imagined for a second standing very still and closing my eyes for a makeover. Then Lexie said, "There she is," and I saw you across the aisle in Ladies' Shoes, waiting near a table covered in jewel-toned pumps.

You nodded at us when we reached you. Then you waved over the salesman who was straightening the sparkly sandal display. He wore a light gray suit with a windowpane pattern and had brown skin, laugh lines at the outer corners of his eyes, and dark hair that was speckled with white.

"This is Ronald," you said. "He has worked in the store for more than twenty years. He will teach you how to sell, Catarina, here in Ladies' Shoes. As for you, Lexie"—your face and voice got very stern—"you will work right there."

You pointed at Hosiery, the next department over, where a gray-haired woman was standing near a tall stack of boxes.

"You will help Shelby unpack and put away every one of the stockings in those boxes. You must sort by texture, support level, and toe quality. And of course by size and color. Are you listening? Navy, control top, sandal foot, size E, *sheer* must not be mixed with navy, control top, sandal foot, size E, *ultra-sheer*. I don't want any mistakes when I come back. Do you understand?"

Lexie looked like she'd been told to pick dead bugs off flypaper. She didn't even bother

trying her angel act—she must've known it
had no shot with you. She nodded instead and
walked over to Shelby.

"I will check on both of you later," you told
me. "Now I must make my rounds."

As you walked away I felt a little panicky,
realizing I had to spend the morning with a
complete stranger, learning how to sell to other
complete strangers.

"Come back!" I wanted to cry.

But Ronald had such kind eyes, and such an
intent way of listening, and he was so obviously
obsessed with his profession. I couldn't possibly
stay scared of selling shoes.

"I think first of all, if you're going to work
here—and good for you that you are; it's a
really good experience, and great to start early—
it's important to understand the stockroom," he
told me.

Then, for the first time in my life, I got to
step behind the Shoes counter and through the
curtain hanging back there, into the stockroom.
I had no idea it was so big, so full of shoeboxes
slid into slotted shelving from floor to ceiling.

Plus there's that rickety flight of metal steps, and that whole extra mezzanine level, for boots! I felt like Nancy Drew finding the hidden staircase.

Ronald pointed out where every different kind of shoe is kept and how they're sorted by brand and color and style. He told me which brands are particularly expensive, and which aren't, and which offer very narrow sizes and very wide. I nodded as he talked and tried to take it all in and wondered whether I should ask him to hang on a second so I could try to find paper and pen to take notes, since there was no way I could remember it all.

He was telling me which companies are known for being good to the planet when the store operator sang out over the loudspeaker, "Ladies and gentlemen, the store is now open." We went back through the curtain then to wait for customers.

Before long two women your age showed up and started picking up sneaker samples.

"The woman on the right is Ms. Daniels, size eight and a half," Ronald murmured to me.

"She's with her friend Ms. May. Ms. Daniels will get something, Ms. May won't. Unless they really surprise me."

I followed him over to them, lagging behind a little. I was obviously way too young to be an actual salesperson. I wanted to stand silently a few feet from Ronald and watch him do his thing.

But as soon as he'd greeted those two women, he turned to introduce me. "This is Ms. Gerta's granddaughter Catarina. She's helping me today."

Ms. May frowned a little, looking at me. "I thought her granddaughter was blonde. And more mature-looking."

I frowned back at Ms. May. "I'm more mature-*acting*," I wanted to tell her.

"You're thinking of Lexie," I said instead. "We're cousins."

I glanced into Hosiery, remembering Lexie. She was actually walking my way. When she saw me looking over, she motioned for me to come talk to her.

I shook my head and looked back at Ms. Daniels and Ms. May.

"You're Jacob's girl!" Ms. Daniels was saying.

I nodded and smiled and hoped she'd say something about Dad as a boy.

"We heard you were in town," she said instead. Then she asked Ms. May, "How could we have forgotten?"

"Same way we're always forgetting our sunglasses, I guess." They both started laughing. Ronald joined in politely and, obviously, I should have, too. But I was too distracted by Lexie, who'd moved into my line of sight and was waving hugely with both arms.

I had zero interest in going to her. She was supposed to be working hard at sorting stockings—actually, she was supposed to be *home, punished*—and she definitely just wanted me to help her get to Hank somehow. Maybe stand lookout for them while they met up. I was so sick of Hank. Hank, Hank, Hank, Hank, Hank. How much trouble was she willing to get into for him?

"Would you like me to bring you those sneakers in your size?" I asked Ms. Daniels. The stockroom at least felt safe from Lexie.

"That'd be wonderful," she said, handing me the pink shoe.

As I headed behind the counter with it, I heard Ms. Daniels say, "I remember Jacob helping me find pumps for my son's wedding. Navy satin, not too high in the heel, a rhinestone bow at the toe. Now, that was a beautiful shoe."

It was such a funny feeling, walking through the stockroom curtain while imagining Dad walking through that same curtain, years ago, looking for a pair of shoes for the same woman, years younger.

I stood in the spell of that feeling. Not for long, though. Someone started tapping me hard on the shoulder, making me jump and drop my sample shoe. It was Lexie—the stockroom wasn't remotely safe from her. I got ready to tell her to go away, go back to work, I didn't even want to hear whatever scheme she'd come up with. But then she said, "Come *on*! Safta's sick!" And we both started running together, to find you.

We sprinted past Ronald and Ms. Daniels and Ms. May—all of whom looked pretty shocked as we blew by. "Cat has to take a break!" Lexie yelled, and I added, "Sorry!" We raced past Hosiery and Cosmetics and the two Jewelries—Costume and Fine—and up the escalator. First Lexie, then me. Both of us so worried.

"My friend Gabby's here shopping—she stopped to tell me," Lexie called over her shoulder as we ran through Drapes. "She saw Safta on a mattress in Bedding. With people all around her—Gabby said she'd fainted."

We finally reached Bedding. I looked for you, for a crowd surrounding you, maybe even for paramedics. But the department was basically empty. Just a saleswoman plumping the pillows on a bed display and a customer hugging a throw blanket.

We hurried to the saleswoman. "What happened to Ms. Gerta?" Lexie asked.

"False alarm!" The saleswoman—Brenda, according to her name tag—beamed at us. "She gave us a scare, though! She sat down suddenly right here." She pointed at the display bed. "I thought she looked pale, and she's never sat on the display before, in all the time I've worked here. Usually she tells me it needs straightening. But this time she was rumpling it! So I rushed right to her, and Mrs. Morris over there did, too. But your grandmother insisted she was fine—she just wanted to test the mattress."

"So she didn't faint?" Lexie asked.

"No, no fainting," Brenda said. "Don't worry, really. She got up right away and told me to stop being lazy and get back to work. Doesn't that sound just like her?"

"It definitely does," Lexie said. "I'm going to kill Gabby."

She seemed fully satisfied with Brenda's report. To be a hundred percent honest, I was, too. I'm so sorry about that. I should've done a better job of worrying.

After we'd talked to Brenda, Lexie glanced at her watch and pulled on my hand. "Let's take the back route."

We walked by the Beauty Salon and Travel and Watch Repair, where a woman hunched over a desk, studying something. We'd passed the Cafeteria, which smelled like sizzling bacon, and Gift Wrap, too, when we saw you. You were walking alone out of that door marked DO NOT ENTER. You behaved so strangely! So secretively. After locking the door behind you, you turned quickly and looked all around. When you saw me and Lexie watching you, you actually looked frightened—even though we're your grandchildren! You took a half step back and gripped your key close to your heart. Like you were worried we might take it. Then your face turned stern.

I expected you to say, "Why are you on this floor? Why aren't you working? I told you both exactly where to be."

I got ready to explain that we'd run to check on you.

Before I could speak, you said fiercely, "I don't want you going through this door, do you understand? Either one of you. This door is not for you."

"I know," Lexie said. She widened her eyes and added, in a super-innocent voice, "I couldn't get in if I wanted to. You keep it locked all the time."

I knew then—I *knew*—from those widened eyes and that too-innocent voice: Lexie had already been through that door.

You looked at her closely. But then you shook your head and told us both, "Go back to your departments." I could feel you watching as we walked away.

"What's through that door?" I asked Lexie as we headed down a ramp to the back stairs.

She rolled her eyes. "Nothing. Just a stupid, tiny storeroom with boxes full of papers and old photos." She looked at her watch again and started walking faster. "I risked my life getting that key copied, for *nothing.*"

Questions rushed through my head: *What kind of papers? Who's in the photos? What do you mean, "risked your life"? When? How?*

But before I could ask anything, Lexie sped down the stairs to the bottom, then threw her arms around a boy waiting there.

Did you ever actually see Hank? I know you saw Lexie climbing into his car, but did you ever see *him*? Because the thing is, he is *not cute*. His eyes are too small, his nose has a weird bump in the middle, he has pimples on his chin, his hair sticks up on the right, and he chews gum with his mouth open. I do *not* know *what* Lexie sees in him. He's tall and kind of football-y; maybe she likes that? I have no idea.

Lexie didn't even bother introducing me. She just kind of clung on him, and he grinned a sideways grin and popped his gum, and it was disgusting.

"He has to get out of here," I told Lexie. "Someone's going to see you and mention it to Safta, then she'll tell your parents, and they'll be furious."

"She's right," Lexie said to Hank. Which gave me a second of hope—maybe I'd made her see reason; maybe she'd get him out of the store. But no. "Let's go hide you, and I'll bring you things. Like candy."

"Sounds fun," he said. Then he actually dangled his gum out the side of his mouth.

"That is *not* a good plan," I told Lexie. "You're supposed to stay in Hosiery."

Lexie rolled her eyes. "I cannot sort another stocking packet. It's too boring. You go back— cover for me."

Before I could even respond, she pulled on Hank's arm and started running, and he ran with her, and they left me all alone on the back stairs.

I had a weird flash of memory then, remembering Blondie and Glitter running away from me, down the hallway near Spanish, looking like they were having so much fun, leaving me behind. Why was I always the one left behind?

To make myself feel better, I slid my phone out of my pocket and sent a quick text to Max:

> Remind me never to chew gum
> with my mouth open.

The stairwell let out at a bunch of offices and soda machines, and for a while I couldn't figure out how to get back to Ladies' Shoes. A woman behind the counter in Layaway pointed me in the right direction. Once I'd made my way to the main aisle, I kept looking around for places Lexie might be hiding Hank—behind a suitcase display in Luggage? In a corner of Books? I didn't see them anywhere.

"Look who's back from her break!" Ronald said, smiling, when I finally returned to him. He was measuring a little girl's foot on a black-and-silver foot-measuring contraption. She was super adorable, with auburn curly hair, but she kept lifting her foot up and setting it back down, lifting it up and setting it down.

"Gracie!" her auburn-headed mom called to her from Children's Shoes. "Hold still for the nice man so we'll know what size to get you."

"You want Catarina to show you how?" Ronald asked Gracie.

She looked at me with big brown eyes and nodded.

That's why Ronald was measuring my foot when you arrived.

I was focused on Gracie when you got there, telling her I'd always wanted curly hair. Your voice startled me.

"Is Catarina a good worker?" you asked Ronald.

"Very," he said. Which was nice of him, given my extremely long break. Then Gracie and I switched places, and he measured Gracie's foot.

You pulled me a few steps away.

"Where is your cousin?" you asked, your voice much sterner. "She is not in Hosiery."

"Ummmm." I felt myself get sweaty, just trying to come up with a lie. "I think she got hungry and went to get some candy, just, you know, for energy. So she could work better. I'm sure she'll be back any second."

Then I realized what I'd done—Lexie had actually been talking about getting candy for Hank—what if she'd brought him there, and you went to find her, and you found them both instead?

"Actually, bathroom!" I said really quickly, my face definitely flushing. "She didn't say candy. She said bathroom."

You raised your eyebrows.

I glanced all around, hoping, hoping, hoping to see what I actually did see—Lexie in the aisle, heading our way. But not nearly fast enough.

"Lexie!" I cried, pointing big at you. "Safta's here! I told her you'd be back from the bathroom soon! And there you are, coming back from the bathroom!"

I don't know how you reacted to that ridiculousness—I had zero interest in seeing it. I kept my eyes on Lexie, who finally started hustling.

"Sorry about that," she said when she reached us, not actually looking remotely sorry; looking energized instead, like she'd been on an adventure. "When you gotta go, you gotta go."

You pointed at her. "There will be no more going for you. Your parents will be here soon. We are all having lunch together. You will stay in Hosiery, sorting stockings, until they arrive. Do you understand?"

Lexie made her face very serious. "I do."

You left us then, and it's possible you believed her. I didn't.

"Where is he?" I asked. "Where's Hank?"

Lexie's face lit up. "In that weird room with the papers and photos, with the DO NOT ENTER door. Isn't that perfect? No one ever goes in there! No one even has the key, except me. No one will find him! It's the perfect hiding place. I'm so glad we saw Safta coming out of there, otherwise I might not have thought of it."

My mouth fell open, and I started shaking my hands at her, and for a minute I couldn't speak. When I finally could, I said, "You're *not* the only one with the key! *Safta* has the key! And she *just* said we can't go in there. *No one* is supposed to be in there. The door *says* DO NOT ENTER!"

I *could not* believe her. Hank wasn't supposed to be in the store at all! It was stupid to let him into the secret room. And it was unfair. *I* wanted to get to see what was behind that door. I wanted to read the papers and look through the photos. What was gross Hank doing back there? Probably getting spit-drenched gum all over everything.

"Safta's not a problem," Lexie told me. "We just saw her leave there."

"*So?* That doesn't mean she's not going back. Maybe she wants to look at the papers again. Maybe she forgot her sunglasses in there. Don't you know old women are always forgetting their sunglasses?"

I took my phone out of my dress pocket. "Text him. Tell him to leave that room right now. And leave the store. And send us a picture proving he's out in the parking lot, out of the store entirely."

Lexie was shaking her head. "He can't leave. I locked him in. I had to. That door's always locked, so no one can get in."

She was making me want to pull hair out of my head in chunks. "Do you hear what you just said? *No one is supposed to get in.* That includes Hank! He needs to get out!"

Lexie was looking at me kind of fondly. "The space between your eyes gets all crinkly when you're angry. Did you know that? Right there."

She pointed right above my nose.

"Give me the key," I growled at her. "Give me the key right now."

"I'll go get him," she said. "I told him I'd

bring him some chocolate-covered gummies. He loves those."

"You *can't* go get him! Your parents are coming! And Safta specifically told you not to go anywhere! Give me the key."

Lexie slowly took a ring of keys from her pocket, slid one of them off, and handed it to me.

"Tell Ronald I need another break, and that I'm sorry," I told Lexie. He was still helping Gracie and her mom.

Lexie nodded. "You should bring Hank some chocolate-covered gummies," she said as I started walking away.

Not likely, I thought.

Then I went to your secret storeroom.

It felt like forever before I could go inside. First a woman brought three enormous toys to the Gift Wrap counter and wanted all of them wrapped for her niece's birthday. Then she couldn't decide on a wrapping paper—she didn't want it to be too babyish, because her niece had decided she was a big girl now; but she also didn't want it to be too adult and boring, either. She sounded like the nicest aunt on the planet, but I wanted to shout at her, "Pick a paper! Any paper! It's the thought that counts!"

I didn't actually yell at a customer, don't worry. I stayed by the DO NOT ENTER door, pacing awkwardly, getting angrier and angrier at the thought of Hank inside, snooping through your papers and photos, probably writing ranked lists of his girlfriends on them. Hottest to least hot. Most likely to buy him chocolate gummies.

The moment Best Aunt Ever finally walked off with her bags of wrapped toys, I looked all around to make sure no one else was coming. Then I unlocked the door, let myself in, and quickly shut it behind me.

Why'd you keep everything in such a small space? That beaten-up wooden table to the left, and boxes stacked up and down the wall to the right. Everything was very clean, but so old. The space smelled a little musty, like a used bookstore, but also lemony, like maybe the table had just been polished. The white walls looked dingy and the yellow linoleum floor had to have been there forever. Spots were bubbling.

I wanted so badly to walk over to the boxes and start opening them. I wanted to read everything inside. I needed to figure out what you were hiding in there, why you kept it all locked away in this musty room, why you were so serious about no one else going in.

But, of course, I had to deal with stupid Hank.

Turns out, there was no need to worry about him getting anywhere near anything involving paper. He was sitting on the floor with his back against the wall and his legs stretched out, playing a video game on his phone and blowing bubbles with his gum. He didn't bother looking up.

"You took long enough," he said, pressing, pressing, pressing buttons on his game.

"You have to get out of here," I told him.

He looked up then. "Oh," he said. "It's you."

Then his phone made some crash-and-burn noises. He looked back at it and said a bad word that I won't repeat because you wouldn't like it. "I was about to get a top score." He slid the phone into his jeans pocket and stayed where he was. "Did you bring my candy?"

"No, I did not bring your candy!" He was like a four-year-old—candy, candy, candy. (Actually, I wished he was four—I liked Gracie a lot better than him.) I was keeping half an ear on what was happening outside. I knew you could come back any second. I had to get him out of there.

"Lexie didn't tell me you were cute," he said then, giving me that stupid half grin. "Want to see my car?"

I should've said, "Yes! Let's go see your car!" That would've gotten him out of your room right then and there. But I was so startled and disgusted—I was *Lexie's cousin*! Why would I go with him to his car? All I could say was "*No*. I don't want to see your car."

"It's a red Dodge Charger with a sunroof," he told me. Like I had any idea what a Dodge Charger was. And like a sunroof was some great, rare attraction. "Seat warmers, too."

It's a hundred degrees out, you idiot, I thought. *I don't need my seat warmed.*

Then he *winked* at me.

That was it.

"Does *Ally* like your seat warmers?" I tried desperately to think of all the other girlfriends' names the Piggly Wiggly guy had listed "alphabetically" on the phone. "How about *Deb*? And *Helen*? Do they like your seat warmers?" I knew there were others, too—I couldn't quite remember them. Was one of them Faith?

It didn't matter. Hank seemed panicked just hearing those three. His pimply white chin was looking sweaty—his forehead, too.

"How do you know about them?"

"I know plenty," I told him. Very convincingly, too. I glared at him, listing it all in my head:

I know you're bad news. I know you think you're a whole lot cooler than you are. I know you need better skin care. I know if you keep lying to a bunch of girls, you're going to get caught.

What I don't know is why Lexie wants to spend one second with you.

"If you don't get out of the store right now,"
I told him, "I will tell Lexie *everything*."

That's all it took. He got up, ran his hand
through the sticking-up side of his hair, trying
to look all cool, then pushed past me and out
the door. It occurred to me too late that someone
might see him—I peeked out really fast right
after he'd gone; thankfully there was no one
around. I shut the door and leaned against
it, looking around the room. I felt very tempted
to forget everything else and start opening
boxes.

But a voice in my head was saying, *You have
to go check on Hank! What if he didn't actually
leave the store?* And then, outside my head, the
store operator announced, in her singsongy
voice, "Catarina Arden-Blume, please report to
Hosiery. Catarina Arden-Blume, please report
to Hosiery."

So I had to leave without checking a single
box. I poked my head out the door again, made
sure the coast was clear, locked the room quickly,
and hurried to Hosiery.

I know I did the right thing, scaring Hank away from Lexie. It was so clearly the best choice for her. The only problem was, it made her miserable.

When I met all of you in Hosiery, she was looking all around, obviously hoping Hank would be skulking nearby. She gave me a questioning look; I shrugged to say that I didn't know where he was. And I actually didn't—I hadn't seen him after I'd hurried out of the room.

Lexie scanned the parking lot, too, as we walked to Aunt Miriam's SUV. I knew she was searching for a red Dodge Charger with a sunroof. At that point I still had no idea what a Dodge Charger looked like (I definitely know now—I'll get to that later), but it was easy to tell from Lexie's disappointed face that Hank's car wasn't there.

In the SUV she scooted down really low in her seat and motioned for me to scoot down too. Then she whispered, "What did Hank say to you in the room? Did he say where he was going?"

Maybe I should've whispered back, "He told me I was cute and wanted to show me his seat warmers." And told her about Ally, Deb, and Helen. It would've saved her a very bad moment later.

But she was already looking so upset about him. I didn't want to make her feel worse. And it's not like we could've had that whole conversation—"Your boyfriend has lots of other girlfriends! And I think he likes me!"—with her parents sitting in the front seat. Especially given how angry they'd be just hearing that Hank had met Lexie at the store.

So all I whispered to Lexie was, "I told him he had to get out of there, and he did. Then I locked up. I don't know where he went."

Lexie didn't say anything else. She stayed slumped in her seat and watched out her window for the rest of the ride to the barbecue restaurant.

She barely ate any of her lunch. "But you love the beef brisket sandwiches here!" Uncle Bob said near the end of the meal, when he noticed most of her food still sitting on her plate. "The cornbread, too! Eat up, or I'll have to eat it all for you."

She just pushed the plate toward him. He

shot a worried glance at Aunt Miriam, who shrugged and wiped her mouth with her napkin. I'm guessing she was thinking, *That's just Lexie faking symptoms again.*

I have to be honest, I got pretty annoyed as the afternoon went on and she didn't snap out of it. Lexie was usually the most resilient person on the planet! But in our room she got gloomier and gloomier, sitting on her window seat, looking out at her climbing tree. It was like she was Rapunzel, sitting around, waiting to throw down her hair for the prince. Except it wasn't a prince; it was stupid Hank.

I tried to ignore her. I texted Max.

> Have you ever done the right thing, but the person you did the right thing for doesn't realize it was the right thing—she very wrongly thinks it was the wrong thing—and then you have to deal with her getting all mopey about it?

After a pause he wrote back.

I ate the last piece of my mom's birthday
cake once, and she got mopey because
she'd been saving it for herself.

That did not seem applicable at all.

In what way did you do the right thing?

I was hungry and it was delicious and she
hadn't left a note saying Do Not Eat.

This was appalling. Obviously no one had
ever taught him the rules of cake.
I listed some:

Rules of Cake:

1. Never lick cake frosting off
someone else's fork.

2. If there are vegetables of any kind
in the batter, do not call it cake. (This
includes carrots. Carrot cake is not a
cake. It is a disappointment.)

3. A birthday cake belongs to the
birthday person. DO NOT EAT ANY
OF IT WITHOUT PERMISSION. Even
if there's no sign saying Do Not Eat.

After a second he wrote, Are there rules for cookies?

Yes. Cookies must always be
chocolate chip. Unless Safta baked
her butter cookies, in which case
they're allowed to be butter.

What about oatmeal raisin?

NO! Oatmeal is for breakfast.
Raisins are a dried-up fruit. FRUIT
DOES NOT BELONG IN COOKIES.

No need to get so worked up about
raisins. Maybe you should go smash some
plates. Get all the aggression out. Like the
Greeks do.

What are you talking about?

Smashing plates is a thing here,
apparently. We're going to try it soon.

Let me know if you think it would
help with cookie anger.

Will do.

I thought Lexie might ask who I'd been texting with, but she was still slumped on the window seat, looking outside.

I went to the bathroom, to put a little distance between me and her gloom.

When I came back, she was hunched over,
staring down into her lap. I wanted to say,
Enough already! She sighed and spoke first. "I
don't understand why he's doing this."

"*I* don't understand why you're so miserable," I told her. "So he didn't say goodbye to you
at the store—so what?"

"I texted him," she said. "He said he needs to
take a break."

"What?" I had no idea how that could've happened. "When did you text him? And how? You
don't have your phone."

Of course—*of course*—she held up *my* phone, which she'd set in her lap.

"Where'd you get that?!"

"You left it on your bed while you were in the bathroom."

"But I have a password. How'd you send a text?"

She shrugged. "I grabbed it fast, while it was still on."

I went and snatched it back from her.

"Did you read my texts?" I asked, glaring. I felt weirdly ready to pull her hair, hard, if she'd seen my conversations with Max. Not that there was anything bad in them. But they were mine.

She shook her head. "I didn't have time to read them. You came back too fast."

I believed her, especially since she'd pretty much admitted that she would've read my texts if she could've.

I read hers. (The ones she'd sent on my phone.)

Lexie: Hey, it's Lex. Come meet me at the store again tomorrow am. I'll be there with my cuz.

Hank: Can't.

Lexie: Maybe next day?

Hank: Text me when your cousin's gone.

Lexie: She doesn't care if I'm with you instead of her.

Hank: I need a break. I want some space. Text me then.

I would not have thought it possible to like that boy even less, but now I did. He "needed a break" just long enough to make sure I didn't actually tell Lexie what a bucket of oozing slime he was. Then he'd go right back to sliming.

Again I thought about telling Lexie how cute he thought I was, along with every other girl he'd ever seen.

But it's just really hard to say that kind of stuff. I decided maybe it wasn't necessary—maybe Lexie'd forget about him, or somehow realize she deserved way better, if she had time away from that intestinal worm.

"I think it's good to take a break," I told her. "Think things over. You're punished anyway. Maybe it's better not to take risks with your parents."

She looked all sad again. "You don't understand." She shook her head. "I don't want to talk about this anymore—let's talk about something else."

"Sounds great to me," I said. But then I couldn't think of a single other topic.

I was still holding my phone. She glanced at it and, with at least a little life to her voice, said, "How come you never talk about your friends?"

I assumed she meant Max, and I wanted to hurl something heavy at her. "You *just* told me you didn't read my texts!"

"I didn't read them," she said calmly. "I looked at your pictures. Give me the phone—I want to show you something."

"No." She was never getting my phone again. She was the sneakiest, most impossible person on the planet.

Except, which pictures did she mean?

"Just give it to me," she said. "I'm only going to show you what I've already seen."

"Fine," I said. It's not like I had anything too secret.

"Look at all these pictures of you with these two girls." She was showing me, of course, pictures of Blondie and Glitter. The three of us each wearing the "Ruthie!" sweatshirts that

Ruthie had given out as party favors at her bat mitzvah. (I lost mine a long time ago, thank goodness, so I don't have to figure out how to burn it.) The three of us with chocolate mustaches, drinking hot chocolate near school. The three of us holding up a poster—done a hundred percent *by me*—for our Spanish presentation on traditional clothing in Spain. (We'd gotten an A on it. We were happy.) Etc., etc. The pictures went on and on.

"Okay, I get it." I grabbed back my phone.

"Then they just end," Lexie pointed out, entirely unnecessarily. "Those girls aren't in any of your later pictures. What happened?"

How could she be so clueless about Hank, and like a genius bloodhound about everything else?

"You don't want to talk about Hank, and I don't want to talk about that," I told her. "Let's talk about something else."

"Why don't you want to talk about it?"

"It's just a long story."

"Good." She pointed at the other half of the window seat. "Sit. Tell it."

I hadn't told anybody the whole story of

Blondie and Glitter yet. It was upsetting and mystifying, and I didn't want to relive it.

"Come on," she said. "We're both stuck here. I can't watch TV or use my own phone, Mom's taken every single electronic, and Hank wants a break, and I have no idea why. I'm just going to be sad and bored while you read one of your thousands of books. Tell me the story instead. Please."

I felt a little responsible for her Hank pain. So I decided to give in.

"Fine." I sat facing her on the window seat, both of us leaning against opposite walls with our feet stretched out, and I told her all of the Blondie and Glitter drama. Everything from "There's Cat! *Run!*" to "We're going to do our project on Picasso, so *ha!*"

Lexie can be a really good listener when she's interested and not on her phone. Or mine.

"I hate them," she said. "They're terrible people. At least that guy Max is nice. And good thing school's over, so you're not stuck with those atrocious girls anymore."

"I'm supposed to be stuck with them right now, actually. We'd signed up for a bookmaking camp in the West Village together. I came here instead."

She looked outraged. "But you love books—it's *weird* how much you like them! And instead of getting to make them, you're stuck here measuring people's feet and finding shoe sizes. That's so not right."

She got that look she gets when she's scheming—her eyebrows went down a bit and her eyes glazed.

"What are you thinking about?" I asked.

She blinked, shaking herself out of that zone. "I have to figure out how to prove to those two that you're having a way better time without them. They don't need to know the truth."

"I *am* having a way better time without them."

"Right." She laughed when she said it, like it couldn't possibly be true. Then she went back into her zone.

But it *was* true. And not just because being with those two was basically unbearable. I liked lighting candles with you and walking through the curtain into the shoe stockroom—the same curtain my father used to walk through—in

my family's store. I liked seeing all the hidden
parts of the store—the ramp to the back stairwell, your secret storeroom. I wanted to look in
those boxes. I liked that everyone in the store
thinks I'm special because I'm connected to
you. I liked pinning on my employee name tag.
I liked knowing Rose-Marie and learning Louisiana Creole words and talking with Lexie on her
window seat. I liked feeling part of something
other than just me and my mom and my dad
in our apartment. I felt a little different now,
like I had the same outline I'd always had, but
there was more filling me up. I couldn't have
explained it to Lexie—I wasn't sure I'd fully figured it out myself. I was glad she didn't ask.
But even stuck at home with her while she was
punished, even spending the morning dealing
with people's feet, I was still having a pretty
good time.

Days passed after that, and we fell into a routine. Aunt Miriam dropped us every morning at the store, and you assigned us departments near each other. I sold clutches and mini designer backpacks in Handbags; Lexie sold lip glosses and bronzers in Cosmetics. I cleaned glass displays in Fine Jewelry; she sorted trench coats by size and color in Outerwear. I handed out flyers for the Bayou Country Music Jam in Local Happenings; she told me, every single time she passed, that she should get to go to the jam, it wasn't fair, her parents should ease up on her punishment, she'd been good for so long. She also gave away samples of chocolate truffles in Candy.

I'm guessing this won't shock you: Lexie was away from every one of her assigned departments way more than she was in them. Somehow she almost always managed to get back just before you arrived to check on us.

She tried to get me to come with her on a gazillion breaks. "Come *on*," she'd say. "Come with me. This is boring." But I only took a few a day. I enjoyed learning about the different departments, and having employees and customers tell me they'd known my dad when he was young. Some of them said I had his smile—I liked that especially. Plus I didn't want you coming by, not seeing me, and thinking I didn't care.

I did go on breaks with Lexie at least once in the middle of each morning. We wandered around the store together, trying to take fun pictures on my phone to post online. This was part of Lexie's master plan to get back at Blondie and Glitter—she wanted me to be able to prove I was having an amazing summer without them. We took pictures of ourselves getting makeovers in Cosmetics and driving the giant battery-operated car in Toys and wearing matching satiny bridesmaids' gowns in Bridal. Maybe it should've felt faked, but it always ended up actually being fun.

We took another break for lunch every day, too, and headed to the Cafeteria for milkshakes and grilled cheese or burgers or turkey clubs. Charlie behind the counter started a chocolate milkshake for Lexie and a vanilla one for me as soon as he saw us coming. LuLu made us sandwiches with pickles and chips. Then, usually, while we sat and ate, Lexie went on and on about Hank.

"I don't understand why he ditched me—do you?" Every single lunch she said that, or something very similar. "I *have* to figure out where Mom hid my phone. I cannot *wait* until I get it back. Do you think he's texting me on it? He hasn't texted me on your phone, has he?"

I sipped my milkshake, and shook my head or nodded at the right moments, and tried not to show that I knew exactly why he'd ditched her.

Then there was the thing we did after lunch every day. That's what I'm most ashamed of now. Because every day we snuck back into your secret room.

Actually, I was the one who snuck in. Lexie had zero interest in being in the room without Hank.

"There's literally nothing interesting in there," she told me when I said I wanted to go back in. "The Flatware department is more fun."

"I just need you to stand guard and knock

three times fast if you see Safta," I told her.

"That I'll definitely do." Once she sniffed danger, she was all in.

Every day we looked very carefully all around and made sure no one was nearby or paying attention. Then I unlocked the DO NOT ENTER door and slipped inside while Lexie kept watch.

I knew I couldn't stay in there too long. I never wanted you to find me. As soon as I was inside, I looked at my watch, then went to a box and started lifting things out and taking pictures of it all, as quickly as I could. When ten minutes had passed, I left.

You'd be surprised how many pictures of documents and old photographs can get taken in ten minutes. Every time I went, I got through a lot.

And every afternoon, when we were back in our room at Lexie's house, I studied it all. First the pictures, each black and white, with people's names written on the back in your neat and curly handwriting. You wrote "Gerta" on some, so I learned what you looked like as a girl. Dark haired, like me, with a big smile and laughing eyes.

That hit me hard, seeing you full of joy like that. Because I couldn't imagine it now.

One of the pictures looked like it had been folded very small, then unfolded again. It showed another girl, about my age. Her face was rounder than yours, her nose wider, her eyes bigger. She looked worried, like she needed something but doubted she'd be able to find it. On the back of the photo you'd written "Addy." I wondered who she was and why the picture had been folded. Had you carried it in a pocket?

I read a bunch of the papers, too. Not just the ones in English. I spent hours trying to figure out the ones in German, looking up words online, using a translation app, doing my best. I couldn't get through every document, but for a lot of them I'm pretty sure I got the gist.

You'd kept a million yellowing letters from places like the American Red Cross, the Jewish Agency, and the Hebrew Immigrant Aid Society. From German organizations, too. The ones I read responded to your requests for information about the whereabouts of many people, all Jewish, all from one town in Germany.

Sometimes the letters said versions of "We

regret that at this time we have insufficient information." Sometimes they said, "We regret to
have to share the news that she perished," and
then they'd name a place and a date.

Sometimes—rarely, but sometimes—you got
good news. Someone had been found.

You must've sent letters to all of those found
people. I can't know for sure, because there
were no copies of what you sent. I do know you
got responses from some. They're in German,
and I couldn't find translations for every word,
but they all seem to be thanking you for offering them a job if they wanted to come to America. Offering to be their sponsor.

They all say thank you. They all say you've
given them hope.

I realized pretty quickly that you were trying to find victims of the Holocaust and help
them if you could. I knew about the Holocaust
from school. I'd learned that Jews had property
and jobs taken from them; that they were kicked
out of schools; that they were rounded up from
their homes and shot or put on trains and sent to
concentration camps. I'd seen photographs of
the living and the dead in those camps. It was

terrible, indescribable, unbearable. But I could always close the book when I wanted, or shut my eyes during documentaries. Then the school unit ended, and that was it. Even though I'd known I had a grandmother—you—who came to America from Germany during those years, I'd still felt very distant from it. I'd never laid eyes on you. And Dad had always said you wouldn't talk about that time—he never wanted to discuss you, anyway. When I thought about you, I focused on the fight between the two of you. Not on Germany.

Now, though, the obvious finally slammed into me: You were Jewish, and you'd been there, as a girl. What had you seen, exactly; what had happened right in front of you? Were all of these people your friends, your neighbors? Your family—*my* family? Were they rounded up and taken away? How had you been saved?

"What's Safta's maiden name?" I hated having to ask Lexie that. I couldn't fully blame Dad, either. Yes, he'd never told me, but he would've. If I'd bothered to ask.

Lexie was lying on her stomach on the floor near me, feet in the air, flipping through a fashion magazine. She didn't seem to care that I knew so little about you. She just said, "Bresler," then licked a finger and turned a page.

I looked through the list I'd been making on the notepad, keeping track of everyone. I saw many Breslers. Three in the column I'd marked "perished." (I hadn't yet figured out what had happened to the others.)

I got overwhelmed then, sitting on Lexie's floor, surrounded by my laptop and phone and notepad and pen, thinking about you opening letters and learning that members of your family had died. Thinking about you searching and searching for all of these other people, too, writing and writing all those organizations for years. Thinking about everyone who'd vanished forever, and everyone you'd tried to save. Had you opened the store to save them?

"Does anyone really old and German work in the store?" I asked Lexie.

She looked up from her magazine. "You mean other than Safta?"

"Right."

She thought for a second. "I'm pretty sure

Inga Eisenmann in Alterations came from Germany. And the old manager in Men's—he retired a while ago. I can't remember his name. They're both ancient. They go to our synagogue."

"Inga Eisenmann in Alterations!" I said, holding up the notepad, waving it a little in the air for her, pointing at Inga's name on the list. "She's one of the people who made it! That's got to be her! And I know her, right? She altered my clothes!"

I'd only met her once, and I'd done nothing at all to help her leave Germany; but it felt pretty great anyway, knowing you'd done it— you'd gotten at least one person to safety in America after something horrible. And she was still around now, working in your store.

Lexie was looking at me like I was an alien.

"I have no idea what you're talking about," she said. "And I have to teach you what's actually exciting. It's definitely not alterations."

"No—really—you have to listen to this," I said.

Then I told her everything I'd been learning. I thought she might already know about the family members. But she didn't know about anyone or anything. "No one ever talks about Germany," she told me.

I thought she might be surprised, too, about one thing: You were always so mean and bossy around us, and those papers showed how good and generous you could be.

But she said, "This reminds me of the story about Ms. Diaz, the Ready-to-Wear buyer. Have you heard it?"

I shook my head.

"I used to ask Mom to tell it all the time." Lexie shut her magazine and sat up cross-legged. "One day, long, long ago, Safta was in Luggage, doing one of her rounds. A woman walked up to her—a complete stranger—and said, 'Are you Ms. Gerta?'" Lexie made the woman sound very nervous. "'Gerta Blume?'

"'Yes, I am Gerta Blume.'" (Lexie does a great imitation of you.)

"The woman forgot to introduce herself. She just said, 'I have a cousin in Cuba. She and her husband have three little children. The situation is very bad. People are getting captured then shot, one by one, in front of a wall, if they disagree with the government. My cousin and her husband—they disagree with the government. They need to leave, but they are trapped.'

"'You need a form signed,' Safta said.

"The woman nodded and held up a sheet of paper. 'They can leave if someone signs this, saying my cousin has a job here, in America.'

"Without hesitating for one second, Safta said, 'Did you bring a pen?'

"The woman took one out of her purse. Then Safta told her, 'Hand me the paper and the pen and turn around, please.'"

Lexie made a motion with her finger, signaling me to turn around. I didn't understand why, but I did.

"Then Safta signed the paper with the woman's pen, on her back." Lexie held a pretend sheet of paper against my back and signed it with her finger. I imagined approaching a complete stranger and asking her to save someone in my family, and actually feeling on my body the signing of the paper—the proof that I'd succeeded.

"Safta did that for anyone who needed to escape a bad place," Lexie said, as I turned back around. "She signed papers promising them jobs. Even though she'd never met them. And even though she didn't actually have job openings. 'I will pay them to count paper clips, if I have to.' That's what she would say."

I could still feel the signature Lexie had scribbled on my back. How many people had brought you papers, knowing you'd sign?

"It's how Yana in Designers got to the US," Lexie said, as if she'd heard my thoughts. "And Ms. Diaz—she was the Cuban cousin, in the story. Other people, too. It's weird that your dad didn't tell you. My mom loves those stories."

I wished she hadn't said that, but she was right. I got mad at Dad again. This was fully his fault—I couldn't have known to ask, and he should've told me. Yes, you'd done the wrong thing, rejecting us because of Mom. But he still could've told me these nice stories about you.

"I don't get something," Lexie said as I sat there stewing. "Why's she keeping this German stuff secret? Everybody knows she helps people from other countries. Why's she hiding the German papers in a room nobody knows about, not even Mom?"

"Maybe your mom *does* know," I said. Not very nicely. I wouldn't have minded if her mom had kept something from her, the way Dad had kept things from me.

But no. "Mom doesn't remember ever going through that door with the DO NOT ENTER sign," Lexie told me. "She thinks there are nonfunctioning mechanicals back there. Whatever that means. Also, Mom's always said Safta refuses to talk about her time in Germany."

I nodded. Dad had at least told me that. "Dad says the same thing."

"So what actually happened to Safta while she was in Germany?" Lexie asked. "That's what I want to know. Have you seen anything in the boxes about that?"

"Not yet," I said. I hadn't read every word of every document we already had, but I'd made sure to translate anything with your name on it. I was pretty positive there was nothing helpful there. "And I only have two boxes left."

I went to bed early that night and lay awake for a while, thinking. Getting mad at you, actually. I kept wondering—how could you be so overwhelmingly generous to everyone else, doing so much to be kind to them, to save them, and yet be so very mean to my mom? And to my dad, just because he loved her? It was the opposite of generous—it was selfish—to cut all of us out, to punish us, me included, just because we didn't follow one idea you had about what was right. It didn't make any sense. You were a whole lot more caring to strangers than you were to us, and you were supposed to love us.

I turned that over and over in my mind, not getting anywhere, until I fell into a deep sleep. A few hours later, Lexie started shaking my shoulder, waking me.

"Get up!" she hissed in my ear. "Get dressed!"

I sat straight up, eyes wide, heart pounding. "Who is it? What happened? What's wrong?"

"Shh," Lexie whispered. "Everything's fine." She'd raised a window shade; the room was half-lit by streetlamps and the moon. "Here." She handed me my low-riding shorts and one of my tank tops. "We're going to the Bayou Country Music Jam!"

I was still more asleep than awake. I blinked at her, grabbed the clothes, and wiped drool off the side of my mouth.

"Bayou Country Music Jam," I repeated. It took a few more seconds for my head to clear. Then I remembered—we were *not* going to the Bayou Country Music Jam. Aunt Miriam had specifically forbidden it.

Lexie was making "hurry up!" circles with her hand. "Hank's picking us up in ten minutes. I got Gabby to get us three tickets—they're at Will Call—then I texted Hank. I *knew* this would get him to end our break! He loves Slick Billy and the Goatees."

"No," I told her, scooting backward on my bed and shaking my head. "No, no, no. Your mom said *not* to go to this jam. And we're not sneaking off with Hank! He's not worth getting in trouble for! He's taking a break from you, remember?"

"I *knew* you'd go all goody-goody," Lexie said. "That's why I didn't tell you that I called

Gabby and Hank from the phone in Flatware. You have to come! We'll take pictures for Blondie and Glitter—they'll be super jealous."

"No, they definitely won't," I told her. "They *do not* care about the Billy Goats."

"Slick Billy and the Goatees. And they *will* care when they see how much fun we're having! You have to come!"

"I don't. I really don't."

"No, you really do." Her voice was serious now, instead of like a cheerleader. "For some reason Hank only agreed to go if I proved to him you were okay with it. It's totally weird; he seems almost scared of you. So I told him you were *great* with it—you wanted to come with us." She put her hands together like she was praying. "Please, please, please, please, please."

I did *not* want to go. I have never once had even the tiniest desire to sneak off in the middle of the night. Bad things happen to kids who do that. They get kidnapped and locked in concrete basements, and their bodies are only found decades later when new owners move in and discover human bones in the walls during a renovation. Had Lexie never watched a crime show?

Also, I didn't want to think about what Aunt Miriam and Uncle Bob would do if they caught her sneaking out to meet Hank at night, at the Bayou Country Music Jam, where she'd been told not to go, *while she was still being punished* for meeting him in broad daylight at the Piggly Wiggly. How could she possibly take that risk? I didn't want any part of it.

But I didn't want Lexie going alone with that slime-covered cretin, either.

I realized I had to do something I should've done before, to keep us from getting into this mess in the first place. I had to tell her the whole truth about Hank.

"Listen—" I said, looking away from her, trying not to think of all the different ways she was going to be upset. "I should've told you before, but Hank called me cute. In Safta's storeroom the other day. And that other boy at the Piggly Wiggly"—what was his name? I couldn't remember right then—"he said Hank's got lots of girlfriends. Like a million of them."

I waited for a second before glancing back at her. I expected her to launch into angry questions like "What do you mean, he called you cute? And what other girlfriends? Why didn't you tell me all this before?"

Instead she said nothing at all.

When I looked at her, she was *smiling* at me. *Fondly.* Like I was a two-year-old.

"Of course he called you cute," she told me. "You're my little cousin. And yes, he's had lots of girlfriends. He's *fifteen.* He's *popular.*"

I was speechless. She was acting like *I* was the idiot!

I was not the idiot!

Before I could tell her all the ways she was wrong, there was a flash of light out the window.

"That's him!" Lexie said, running to the window and peering out. "He's flashing his headlights—that's our signal. Throw on your clothes, let's go!"

"Fine." I couldn't leave her alone with him. I just couldn't. "Fine, fine, fine."

She bounced on her feet a bit and clapped very quietly. "Hurry, hurry, hurry."

I threw on some clothes and followed her out the window, onto the deck. It was strange being outside at that hour, under the night sky, with the sound of crickets in the distance and the low rumbling of Hank's car beneath us. I felt a funny kind of peace for a second before I looked around and realized: the tree.

"I can't get down that thing," I whispered.

"Of course you can! It's easy. Watch." She walked close to the tree. Then, while I watched in horror, she somehow stood quickly on the deck railing, grabbed a branch, walked her hands along it, and wrapped her legs around the tree trunk. Then she moved down the trunk and sat on a lower branch.

When she was standing on that railing I wanted to shout, "WHAT ARE YOU DOING? GET DOWN!" But I was worried I'd startle her, and she'd plummet through the moonlit darkness to her death.

"I'm not standing on the railing," I hissed at her.

"It's fine!" she hissed back.

"It's not!"

"Try jumping, then. Just jump up and grab a branch."

Of course that didn't work—there's a reason she stood on the railing—those branches are high.

Stupid, snotball Hank flashed his lights again.

"Hang on," Lexie said. "I'm coming back. I'll hold you."

That's how I managed it. Like a baby, I had my older cousin hold my legs while I very, very carefully stood on a railing and grabbed a tree branch.

"Now all you have to do is get close to the trunk and wrap your legs around it," Lexie said.

I hated being in that tree. The bark dug into my hands and I scraped my cheek on the trunk, and then I heard rustlings and I knew a roach could fly into my hair any second and snakes were probably slithering on branches toward me. I scrambled down as fast as I could and ended up missing the last branch, falling, and landing hard on one knee.

"Ow!" I cried, then covered my mouth. The rest of the street was quiet around us.

"Guess you decided you liked me after all." Hank was leaning his sleazoid self out the driver-side window, smiling that creepy half smile at me.

"Believe me," I told him, rubbing my knee. "I didn't."

The stars were bright in the sky, unlike nighttime in Manhattan. "What time is it?" I asked.

"Almost eleven," he said. "That's when the set starts. We gotta go!"

Lexie hopped out of the tree then and landed easily on two feet beside me.

"Took you long enough," Hank told her. "Let's go."

Lexie ran to get in the front seat next to that coughed-up hairball. I limped over and sat in the seat behind her.

"Too bad you can't really see the car in the dark," Hank said, turning to look at me. "She's a beauty."

"Just drive," I told him. There was exactly nothing interesting about the inside of his "beauty." It was just the dark gray interior of a car with matching gray upholstery on the seats. I buckled my seat belt, then double-checked to make sure it was fully clicked. What if he was a stupid and reckless driver, just like he was a stupid and reckless boyfriend? I should've thought of that before I climbed down that roach-infested tree.

"Lexie, put on your seat belt," I told her.

"Okay, Mom." She buckled up and told Hank, "Remember, don't pass Safta's house. Go the other way."

I put my face in my hands and slid down in my seat. I'd forgotten all about how you sometimes spied on Lexie getting into this car. As Hank drove off I turned, still keeping low, and peered out the back window, worried that I'd see a light on in your house, maybe even your face at the window. But it was all very dark and quiet.

About a block later Hank cranked the music loud. Of course. Some song about highballing it down the low road.

"This is them!" Lexie turned and shouted at me. "Slick Billy and the Goatees! Don't you love it?"

"Mmn." That's all I said. But I remembered

kind of liking the Slick Billy song Aunt Miriam had played during our ride to Baton Rouge from the New Orleans airport. Something about missing Ms. Izzy in Mississippi. This highballing one wasn't bad, either.

I have to give Hank credit, too. He blared the music, but he drove carefully. Probably because he didn't want to risk messing up his "beauty."

It wasn't a long drive, either. We had to park a ways from the stadium, but the streets were brightly lit and there were tons of people out, all streaming in the same direction. Lexie held on to Hank's arm, but she also kept an eye out for me, turning every so often, making sure I was still with them. At one point she started jumping up and down, waving an arm, "Gabby! Gabby! Over here!"

A girl wearing a fire-engine red SLICK BILLY AND THE GOATEES T-shirt ran over to us. She had dark, curly hair pulled up in a high bun; brown skin; and wide eyes filled with excitement. "I was just going to meet you at Will Call!" she said. "Come on—follow me!"

It took forever to get our tickets and push through people and find the right gate and section and seats. By the time we arrived, the band was playing. We couldn't really see them onstage, but we could on the giant screens. People all around us were standing and jumping and singing and screaming. Part of me would've rather been in bed, or watching this at home on TV, but it was also fun to see everybody so excited. Also, songs stick with me, especially if I've heard them recently, so I could sing along to the highballing/low road song. Which turns out to be a huge hit with Slick Billy fans. I was totally into that concert during that song.

Hank left after the song finished. He said he was going to the bathroom, then didn't come back for a while. Which was perfectly fine with me, but Lexie kept looking around for him. Finally she shouted at me and Gabby, loud enough to be heard over the music, "I have to go to the bathroom, too. Come with me!"

We bumped past folks on our row, then walked up the lit stairs and past concessions, following the signs for the restrooms. We got to Men's first, unfortunately. I heard Gabby say, "Oh, no." Then I saw Hank right outside the door—definitely Hank, same jeans, same white T-shirt, same pimply profile, same hair sticking up on one side—doing some serious kissing with a blonde girl.

It was like watching an earthworm slither into someone's ear. One hundred percent disgusting.

"Hank?" Lexie said in a weak voice. And then, "*Faye?*"

Faye, I remembered. *Not Faith. Faye.*

Lexie was shaking her head, and her mouth was shut super tight, and I worried that she'd start to cry, right there in front of skanky Hank. She ran next door instead, into the women's bathroom. Gabby rushed after her. I held back for a second. I had some announcements to make.

Hank and Faye had stopped their hanky-panky, so at least I didn't have to see any more of that. And Hank had the decency to look a little guilty. Faye just seemed confused.

"He's got a million girlfriends," I told her. "You're just the letter F to him."

To Hank I said, "From now on I'm telling everybody."

Then I stormed over to the women's bathroom myself.

I found Lexie holding on to the sink, staring into the mirror. Gabby had an arm around her.

"I'm so stupid," Lexie said.

"*He's* the one who's stupid," I told her. "Monumentally stupid. World-record-setting stupid."

"You deserve a million times better," Gabby said. (Lexie obviously has *much* better taste in friends than in boyfriends.)

"I can't stay at this concert," Lexie said. "Not with them here."

"Of course you can't," I said.

"I'll call my dad," Gabby said.

Gabby's dad picked us all up then and brought us home. When we got to Lexie's he waited until we'd gotten safely inside before driving away, so we couldn't use the tree. Thank goodness. Lexie unlocked the back door instead and we snuck in really quietly, which wasn't hard because Lexie hadn't said a word since she'd left the stadium bathroom. When we got upstairs, she didn't bother putting on pajamas. She just slid under her covers fully dressed and turned away from me.

She obviously didn't want to talk. I felt wide-awake, though. I couldn't stop thinking about her face when she saw Hank making out with Faye.

At least it wasn't the middle of the night in Greece. I got my phone and saw that I already had a text from Max. I'd been too distracted to notice.

> Things you learn in Greece: monk seals
> hear better than we do, but they have no
> ears

I wrote back:

> I wish I'd never heard a single word
> said by Lexie's boyfriend. Or seen
> him, either. I cannot even tell you
> how bad he is.

He wrote back right away. As bad as Blondie and Glitter?

> Worse.

> Dios mío that's bad. Get her away from
> him—bring her to Greece!

I'll ask tomorrow if she wants to get
sunburns and break plates.

Smashing plates is great—you can heave
all your bad feelings onto the ground
and watch them shatter. Kind of found
out today it's mostly a tourist thing, but
whatever—it still helps—come and see!
Both of you.

We talked for a while about painting Hank's
pimply face on the plates before smashing
them. Then we said good night.

I had no trouble sleeping after that.

The next morning I had to wake Lexie up.

"It's time for breakfast," I told her. "We can't be late for Safta."

"Go away." She pulled her covers up higher. "I'm not leaving the house today. I'm staying in bed."

"You can't just lie here." I started tapping her on the shoulder. "You need to be distracted. Plus I want you to stand lookout—we have to see what's in the last two boxes."

She didn't move. I shook her a little. She put her pillow over her head. Finally I said, "He's a blowfly! Don't let a blowfly control how you spend your day!"

She lifted the pillow just high enough to see me. "A blowfly?"

"Yes. They're big, black, hairy flies that lay eggs in the flesh of dead animals. Maggots crawl out when the eggs hatch."

"How do you know that?" She was looking deeply disgusted. Which was better than miserable.

I shrugged. "I read about it somewhere."

She put her pillow back over her face, but I yanked it off and pulled on her arm.

"Come on—let's go get some biscuits. You'll feel better after Rose-Marie's biscuits."

"How am I supposed to eat biscuits? You just went on and on about maggots and dead flesh."

She got out of bed, though. We dressed and pinned on our name tags. Looking down at hers as if making sure it was straight, hair hanging in her face, she said, "I hate it that everyone's laughing at me."

"*Who's* laughing at you?" I said. "I'm not. Gabby's not. Nobody who actually likes you is laughing. They're just hating Hank. Believe me. I know."

She still didn't move for a second. "You tried to warn me," she said. "I didn't listen."

I made my face very stern and pointed at her. "Let that be a lesson to you, missy."

She smiled the tiniest bit at that. Then she followed me down to breakfast and was quiet at the table. I don't think Aunt Miriam or Uncle Bob noticed—they were caught up in a conversation about an antique pistol Uncle Bob wanted—but Rose-Marie looked worried. She put an extra biscuit on Lexie's plate and, as she set it down, told her, "You eat up, joli child. You need your strength."

Lexie was quiet in the car, too. As we walked into the store, she told me, "I knew he did this to another girl, before we started going out. I thought I was different. I thought he really liked me."

"He's a cockroach," I told her. "I wish I could smoosh him with my shoe. Do you want me to? I'll find him and stomp on his face. I'd get his spit-covered gum on the bottom of my shoe—but that's okay. I'd do it for you."

She gave me a half smile and stood a little straighter, and we went to find you for our assignments. You put me in Stationery, probably my favorite department in the store other than Books. I love trying out fancy pens on the scratch pad at the counter and flipping through journals, feeling the paper, deciding which ones I want most.

Lexie was supposed to work across the aisle in Luggage, but she spent even less time in her department than usual. I hoped she was finding good distractions.

But around the time we were due for our first break, she came running to Stationery, wild-eyed and panting, like she'd just seen your car care center go up in flames.

"What is it?!" I said. "What happened?!"

She pulled me aside and hissed, "He's *here*!"

"Who? *Hank*?"

"Who else?! Buying chocolate-covered gummies in Candy, the big a—" (You can guess the word.)

I couldn't believe that boy. I wanted to do a lot worse than stomp on his face. "Why would he come here?"

"How should *I* know?! I haven't talked to him! I'm never talking to him again. And I want him out of our store!"

Our store. I felt a quick urge to hug her.

Then a diabolical scheme sprang into my head. As if I was Lexie, in the days when she wasn't thrown off her game by a cheating jerk of an ex-boyfriend.

"I have an idea," I told her. "Come on—let's see if he drove himself."

Sure enough, we found his "beauty" parked right outside, next to a handicapped spot.

"Hurry—we have to do something before he leaves—I'll tell you on the way."

I explained the whole plan as we rushed up the back stairs. Then we ran to the Cafeteria. "We'll take our milkshakes to go today, Charlie," Lexie said when we reached the counter.

"Coming right up," Charlie said. He made the shakes for us and put them in a paper bag. We thanked him, then ran back to the car, and I started pouring my shake on the hood. I thought Lexie would pour hers there, too, but she climbed onto the car instead and dumped hers through the open sunroof, onto the front seat. Right on the seat warmers.

I thought we'd get caught for sure, especially because she looked so weird up there. But it turns out it doesn't take much time to dump two shakes. Only one man passed by while we were out there, and he was staring at his phone—he didn't even notice.

"That was fun!" Lexie hopped off the car grinning, looking like her old self. "Now what?"

I grinned back at her. I'd never mastermineded a villainous plan before. It felt pretty great.

"Now we ask the store operator to make an announcement," I told her.

Back in Stationery, after I'd explained more, Lexie called the operator. "Hey, Shirley," she said. "It's Lexie." They had a little chat, then Shirley made this announcement: "Would the owner of a red Dodge Charger please report to your car? I repeat, would the owner of a red Dodge Charger parked near a handicapped spot please report to your car."

After that we couldn't risk being seen by Hank. Plus we still wanted to know what was in those two boxes. So we went to your secret room.

Before I get into that dark subject, though, let me share this nice news: It's been weeks since we dumped those shakes. And, according to Lexie's sources, Hank's "beauty" still smells like rotten milk.

There were only two boxes left for me to go through in your room. The first had documents, including a letter signed "Papa" that I couldn't wait to translate. I took pictures of everything in there.

The second box was much bigger. I pulled open the flaps and saw no papers from Germany. Nothing at all from the 1940s. Twin navy comforters instead, and a stuffed bear wearing a sweater that said U-HIGH. A folded Houston Astros banner, too, and photos of a boy with a smile like mine, running in a cross-country uniform, playing basketball, and standing in front of the store with his hand raised in a wave. I also pulled out trophies for debate and speech competitions, and a certificate for Excellence in Entrepreneurship.

I set every single thing from that box carefully on the floor, all around me. And I realized what you'd done. Instead of throwing away all of my dad's things, instead of erasing him entirely, you'd boxed them up and put them here, in the room with the secrets that made you sad.

I stood surrounded by it all, trying to imagine a younger you with my younger dad, hearing the news that he'd won a debate or snapping a picture of him outside the store that you'd built.

I started taking pictures myself then. I didn't want to forget what my dad looked like when he was my age. I didn't want the trophies and certificates kept locked and hidden in a secret box forever, either. I wanted some proof of them. Even the comforters mattered. Definitely the stuffed bear.

I was considering taking the bear when I heard a sound to my right—the sound of a key turning. Every single muscle in my body locked up, and I realized I'd been so stupid—I'd forgotten to check my watch—I didn't know how long I'd been in there—probably way too long. I would've tried to scramble and put everything back in the box, then dive under the desk maybe, but I couldn't get my body to move. It didn't matter—it was already too late. As I stared in horror at the door, it swung open, and you looked right at me. Your face lost all its color and mine probably did, too.

You shut the door fast, and when you looked

at me again, it was like you were seeing the worst kind of shoplifter. Like you desperately wanted to call Security.

"I told you never to come in here," you said. "How did you get in?"

A tiny part of me wanted to say, "Lexie copied the key! I didn't do it!" But I wouldn't have ratted her out. Plus I was the one who'd wanted to keep breaking into your room.

I wondered for a second, too, what had happened to Lexie—why hadn't she knocked three times, and stopped you from coming in? Distracted you somehow? I found out later that she'd run to the bathroom.

Mostly I wanted to push rewind and go back to a time when this hadn't happened. That obviously wasn't possible, though.

You kept looking at me like I'd betrayed you. I handed you the key.

"You're like your father." You said it like it was an insult. "You don't listen. About the important things, you don't listen."

I felt a little better after that, actually. I didn't mind being like my father. Plus his way of not listening was marrying my mother. I love my mother. Not to mention that I wouldn't exist without her.

You don't have to keep all this hidden, I wanted to tell you. *What's wrong with what you've done? Nothing.*

But I didn't want you to know how much I'd read and translated.

"I will clean this later," you said quietly. I'm pretty sure you were talking to yourself. To me you said, "Out."

You waited for me to leave, then followed and locked the door behind us.

Lexie wasn't there, which was good. I didn't want you hating us both.

You looked very pale in the hallway outside the room, very frail, the way you had during our Shabbat dinner, when I'd asked where you got your kiddush cup.

"I don't want to ever see you near this door again," you told me. "Now go back to work."

I hesitated. I wanted to hold your arm and walk you to a seat and bring you water and make sure you were okay.

But you repeated, very sternly, "Go to work. We are both going to work."

So I walked past Gift Wrap and toward the escalator. As I got near the Beauty Salon, I heard the sound of running behind me and someone shouting, "We need a doctor here! Is anyone a doctor?"

And I knew.

It was chaos in the store after that. An ambulance came, and paramedics crouched around you, and a big crowd gathered around them, and I couldn't watch, and they took you away on a stretcher, and I don't like remembering any of it.

Lexie grabbed my phone and called Aunt Miriam; Aunt Miriam and Uncle Bob rushed to the hospital; I called my parents; they started trying to book a flight; Aunt Miriam called Rose-Marie and asked her to bring Lexie and me to the hospital, too.

We didn't get to see you there, in the Intensive Care Unit. Not that day, anyway. But you did such a nice thing for me and Lexie. You sent us a message through your heart doctor, Dr. Bergeron. (The name sounded so familiar when she said it. I realized why later—I'd seen it written on the notepad on the little table in your hall.) She came and found us in the windowless waiting room, where we were all sitting silently, worrying. She wore a doctor's coat over black pants and had dark brown skin, white hair, and serious eyes.

Right away she updated us on your condition.

"She's had a heart attack," she said, sounding
straightforward and looking concerned. Aunt
Miriam kind of moaned, and Uncle Bob put his
arm around her. I wasn't surprised; I'd heard
people at the store guessing that. I still gripped
my seat, though—I wasn't sure what it meant.

"We're monitoring her," Dr. Bergeron said.
"She's sleeping now. She very specifically asked
me to tell you that I've warned her for months
that anything stressful could cause this. We had
warning signs; we knew there were blockages;
but she decided against surgery because of her
age. I raised the possibility of retiring and relax-
ing, but she wouldn't hear of it."

Aunt Miriam shook her head. "Of course she
wouldn't." She sounded a little angry and a little
proud.

"She told me to make sure you heard this,
so I will say it again," Dr. Bergeron said. "It was
only a matter of time before this happened. It
could've been any day."

I know why you insisted she say that. I know

you didn't want me blaming myself. I still do, but a lot less than I would've. I'm so grateful to you for that.

Then she told us they weren't sure what would happen next; they were running tests. You'd stay in the ICU for a few days at least, she said, for monitoring and treatment.

I have to confess to you now what I did that night, long after visiting hours had ended and we'd eaten dinner (except no one really ate) and Lexie had fallen asleep. Even knowing how upset you were about my going through your boxes, even though it'd made you sick, I still translated one more letter. The one signed "Papa." I didn't read anything else from that box, not even the documents in English. But that one letter, from my great-grandfather to you, seemed important. And I knew you couldn't see what I was doing. I knew you wouldn't ever have to know. But I want you to know now, when it won't hurt.

I have to admit, too, that I don't regret it. Because it helped me understand you better than anything else ever did.

I spent hours working on the translation,

and I still couldn't get it all. Here's what I understood: It's dated 8 January 1940, five years before the end of World War II. He said you mustn't feel guilty about the people you hadn't saved. You'd warned as many as you could that you had seen Nazis knocking on doors, announcing that Jews must gather in the square, to be loaded onto trucks and driven away. If you'd kept trying to warn everyone, you would've been killed, too, and you might've exposed the Jews you did save, the ones who'd fled and were hiding in the woods just outside of town. You were so young, he said, just a girl of ten, and you'd done so much. No one could have done better.

He was sorry he wasn't together with you as he wrote the letter, but he was *not* sorry he'd put you on the boat to America with his cousin. He was glad you were safe.

He was still looking for your mother and for someone else—a girl called Adelaide. He'd heard your mother was in a work camp; perhaps it wasn't so bad there. He would go find her. He would find Adelaide, too. You mustn't give up hope. He would find them and they would all come together to America, to join you.

You might not hear from him again for a while, he said. He wanted you to think of him when you held the kiddush cup he gave you as you stepped onto the boat. He said again, do not give up hope.

In a postscript he added that there was no news of your dog, Mazel.

I don't know what happened to Mazel. I do know your parents never made it out of Germany. I asked Aunt Miriam at breakfast the next morning what had happened to them. "They didn't survive the war," she said. That's all you would ever tell her. You boarded a boat to America, and you never saw them again.

I asked Aunt Miriam, too, "What about Adelaide?" I hoped she'd know who Adelaide was.

But Aunt Miriam looked at me blankly and said, "Who's Adelaide?"

I shook my head fast and waved that away. "I must be confused," I said.

But I wasn't. I had "Adelaide Bresler" on my list of people I'd seen mentioned in your papers—people you'd been searching for, after the war. I'd assumed she was a distant relative—an aunt, maybe—until I read your father's letter. I hadn't seen anything yet saying whether she'd survived.

I went back upstairs and started going through all the papers from earlier boxes again, checking every single one for any mention of "Adelaide." In a handwritten letter I hadn't translated before, from someone named Herman Knurr, I found answers. He was sorry to bring bad news, he said. He had known your sister, Adelaide, in a camp called Theresienstadt. They were both the same age, both barely teenagers. She had not let him or anyone call her Addy, because that was your name for her. He said they had so little food, so little warmth, such cold winters. She'd worked in the Central Laundry one morning with a shivering fever and cough. She died within a week.

You'd had a sister you called Addy. And you'd lost her, too.

Ever since I read those two letters, I've wondered about you and your sister. Did you share a room? Did she used to sit beside you on your bed? Did she read to you? Make you laugh? Complain to you? Bake butter cookies with you? Did you wear her hand-me-downs? Did you carry her picture, folded very small in your pocket, when you sailed away when you were only ten?

I have these "what if" thoughts sometimes, too,
remembering what your dad said about how
you left Germany:

What if I knew a house was going to burn all
the way down?

What if people I loved were trapped inside?
What if I couldn't get them out in time?
How would that change me?

Mom and Dad arrived the morning after I read the letters, a Friday. They came straight to the hospital, where we were again sitting in the waiting room, worrying and hoping for good news. Mom looked a little hesitant walking in, and I realized she must've wondered whether she'd be wanted, whether it was wrong to come.

I hurried to her and hugged her, to show that I wanted her. Everyone else greeted her warmly, too. If Aunt Miriam and Uncle Bob were worried that seeing Mom would strain your heart, they never showed it.

You should know this, too. I wondered for a second whether Mom should stay out of your hospital room. Since seeing her might be too stressful for you. I decided it'd be worse if Dad headed right back to New York. Which was a definite possibility if Mom was excluded. There's also this, if I'm being a hundred percent honest: She's my mom, and I love her, and I hoped you would change your mind about her if you got to know her.

After everyone had said hello, Mom and Dad asked a lot of questions about how you were doing, then went to find nurses and doctors to ask more questions. They came back and said what we already knew, which was that you were sleeping. You did so much sleeping in that ICU.

We were bored and had nothing to do but worry and wait. At some point we ate yucky salads with wilted lettuce in the hospital cafeteria. Then I remembered what day it was, and I realized exactly what we should do.

"We should get challah and wine and candles," I said. "And say the Shabbat prayers with Safta, if she wakes up. I think she'd like that."

Dad got stern right away. "Why would you say that, Cat?" He gave me a very disapproving look.

But Mom raised a hand and said, "I agree with Cat. That's a great idea. Where would we get the challah?"

"They'll have some at Albertsons," Aunt Miriam said. "I can pick up our challah cover from home, and a kiddush cup and wine. We'll need to buy white candles—I think we're out."

"Don't forget matches," Uncle Bob told her.

"They're not letting us light matches in the ICU." Dad still sounded angry. He must've felt like I was siding against him and Mom, but it didn't feel that way to me. Not knowing what I knew. I hadn't sorted it all out exactly in my head, but by then I believed deeply that we were all on the same team. I wanted to talk it through with him, but I didn't think I ever could. I'd done enough harm stealing your secrets. They were yours, not mine, to share.

"You're right—no matches," Aunt Miriam told Dad, not seeming to notice his anger. "The synagogue has little electric candles. I'll pick up two of those."

She put on her enormous, dark sunglasses and left with her purse, to run those errands.

"I need some help," Mom said, as we cleared our cafeteria table. "I don't know the blessings. I want to be able to say them with all of you."

"I know them," Lexie said, right away. "I'll teach you."

Back in the waiting room, we pulled chairs around a coffee table. Lexie wrote out the sounds of the prayers so they were easy to read. And while two strangers at the other end of the room watched TV, we quietly said the prayers together. Mom and I said them over and over, trying to get them right. Dad helped with the "ch" sound, giving Mom the exact same advice you'd given me. "Clear your throat as you say it," he told her. "Like you have a piece of carrot stuck there."

We memorized those prayers together, Mom and I. We didn't want to have to read from a paper when we saw you.

Aunt Miriam came back eventually and showed us all that she'd gathered.

Not too much later, a nurse told us you were up for a visit. "A short one," she said. "She's tired today."

It wasn't sunset yet, so the timing wasn't perfect. But it was close enough. We took the challah and the candles and the wine, and we followed the nurse to your room.

You were wearing a white-and-blue hospital gown when we walked in. I know you didn't like that. You would have called the fabric "cheapy," if you hadn't been so weak. You were in the hospital bed with the side rails, and there were tubes attached to your arm, but you'd combed your hair and raised the back of the bed so you were more sitting than lying.

We all came in quietly. Aunt Miriam said, "How are you feeling?" And Uncle Bob said, "You had us quite worried!" You nodded at them without saying anything. You looked at my parents.

"I'm sorry you're sick," Dad said. His voice sounded stilted. "I hope you're feeling better."

At this point you were looking solely at Mom.

"We've only met once, many years ago now," she told you. "I'm—"

"I know who you are," you said, in a hoarse voice, cutting her off.

I jumped in then. I didn't want you to feel stress, and I didn't want Mom to feel bad.

"We brought you Shabbat!" I told you. "Mom and I have been practicing prayers."

You raised your eyebrows, like you were interested.

We set everything up, which wasn't so easy, in that little room, with all the machines and the oversize bed and just one rolling table to set things on. Your eyes went from me to Mom and back again as we all said prayers. First over the candles, which weren't as pretty without the flare of light from a struck match and the dusk settling outside your dining room window. Then over the wine in the kiddush cup, which wasn't the one your father had handed you before you left Germany. It was, though, one you'd given Aunt Miriam. Then over the challah, which Dad tore pieces from in the end, passing them around to everyone.

After that, in the same hoarse voice, you said, "I'd like to talk to Catarina."

My blood turned to ice, I felt so scared. How angry with me were you, still? Had I misunderstood Dr. Bergeron's message? Did you blame me after all?

Everyone turned and looked at me. My bones had turned heavy as cement. Aunt Miriam finally said, "Sure, of course, we'll give you the room." They all left, Mom and Dad last of all. Mom squeezed my hand and raised her eyebrows, giving me a chance to say I wanted them to stay. Part of me did, but I shook my head. I needed to talk to you alone.

When they were gone, and the door had swung shut, you motioned me closer.

I approached, still scared. I had to lean farther in to hear what you said. That's how quietly you said it.

"You have my permission to tell them what you found," you said. "When I'm gone. Only then. When I'm gone, you may tell the family."

"You're not going anywhere," I said. That's the part I latched on to. I knew you meant dying, and it made me even more scared than being yelled at about secrets. "You look fine. You can't go."

You smiled at me and said, "Everyone goes."

Then you raised a finger and said, "Your mother."

My mind started racing. What if you said I could tell everyone in the family your secrets except for Mom, who wasn't Jewish? I didn't want to agree to that. But here you were talking of dying. How could I tell you no?

You leaned a little toward me and said again, "Your mother. You must tell her to condition her hair. And encourage her to wear blue. Nothing orange or red. The shirt she has on now—she looks like a traffic cone. You understand?"

I grinned at you. I did understand. My mom was in.

"And you—you must try to dress better. You will wear the clothes I bought for you?"

I nodded.

You leaned back and closed your eyes. I thought you'd fallen asleep; I started to move away. But you said, with your eyes still closed, "They tried to kill all the Jews. All of us, in my town, in my country, in the countries surrounding us. They rounded us up and killed almost everyone. This is why we have an obligation. For Jewish survival. Do you understand?"

"I do," I told you. "I really do." And for the first time, I really did.

It was then that you dozed off. And that night, while the rest of us slept, you died.

I don't want to talk about your funeral. I'm not saying much—just the few things I bet you'd want to know.

I wore the navy dress you bought for me, with the white bands at the bottom of each sleeve and the top of each pocket. The one I wore on my very first morning working at the store, when you assigned me to Ladies' Shoes. Don't worry, Aunt Miriam had gotten it dry-cleaned. It wasn't dirty and it wasn't wrinkled.

I made sure Mom wore blue, too.

You had a gazillion mourners. The line went from your casket (which was very plain pine—the Jewish tradition, I learned—just how you would've wanted it), down the aisle between the pews, through the lobby of the funeral home, and then out the door and around the block. There were so many honoring you. Merry came. Cindy and Dara and Cara and Charlie and LuLu and Elisa, who smells like baby powder—they all came. Ronald came. Inga Eisenmann from Alterations and Yana and Ms. Diaz and your old Men's manager, too. Lexie kept whispering to me, pointing out people you'd saved. Other employees were also there, and Gabby and her parents, and people who said they'd been customers their whole lives. Rose-Marie came. Even the mayor came. He called you "an institution."

Hank didn't come, thank goodness. It would've been weird if he had, even before our milkshake revenge. But Lexie said Gabby told her that he goes a lot fewer places now because he's worried about something happening to his car.

After the funeral home service, we went to the cemetery. There, in the shade of a giant oak tree, we said the mourner's prayer—the Kaddish—which feels to me like a song. It's caught in my head still. The beginning, at least: *Yitgadal v'yitkadash sh'mei raba.* I thought you might like to know that. I'm carrying a little piece of a Jewish blessing around in my head.

Lexie and I went for a short walk after the funeral, just to get out of the house, which was feeling unusually darkened that afternoon, like it had its own sadness. Rose-Marie met us at the door when we got back.

"A package arrived for you, joli Cat," she told me. "I left it on your bed."

"For me?" That didn't make sense. Who would send me something at Lexie's? Mom and Dad were already in Baton Rouge.

Lexie started hustling upstairs.

"It's not yours!" I shouted, then hurried after her.

She was holding the package when I got to our room. A big brown box, addressed to Cat Arden-Blume c/o Lexie Rosenfeldt, from a Max van Helmond at a hotel in Greece.

"Who's Max van Helmond?" Lexie demanded. "Is that the Max who was so nice to you in Spanish?"

I nodded and took the box, which wasn't heavy, from her. I'd never told Lexie that Max and I were texting. I didn't want to deal with her teasing, and asking if he was cute, and not listening when I said we were just friends.

"Was he in your pictures?" Lexie reached out her hand, palm up. "Let me see your phone."

I ignored her and took the box and my phone to the bathroom and locked the door.

"You're gonna have to show me what's in there!" Lexie shouted down the hall. "That box is too big to hide!"

I knew that. I just wanted to have a second with it by myself.

I knew why Max had sent me something, too. After you went into the hospital, he'd been texting, and I'd been texting back when I could, letting him know what was happening and that I was feeling sad. I knew he was trying to cheer me up.

I pulled the tape off the package and opened it. The box was half-full of packets of minty Greek gum. When I dug beneath them, I found two white plates wrapped in bubble wrap. There was a card, too. "No chewing with mouth open," it said. "And I'm hoping smashing these might help."

I smiled and sat on the tile floor and started texting.

Thanks for my plates and my
lifetime supply of chicle menta.

De nada.

I told him a little about the funeral.
Then, with the *yitgadal v'yitkadash* blessing
playing in my head again, I wrote,

I think I have to have a bat mitzvah.

We'll put chewed up orange gumballs in everyone's
hair! he wrote back. Which made me laugh. It
felt like it'd been a million years since Hannah's
bat mitzvah.
Then he wrote, You can have a loukoumades
station!

A louko-what?

Loukomades. They're Greek donuts. They're
delicioso.

I asked if they had fruit goop inside, or
veggies of any kind, and he said no. So I agreed

to consider including them at the bat mitzvah. But your butter cookies are the only dessert I want there.

After I'd finished texting Max, I brought the two plates to Lexie and led her back outside, to the sidewalk in front of the house. Then I raised one plate high in the air, and she raised the other, and together we hurled them to the ground as hard as we could. (We swept up afterward, don't worry.)

We were still sad after that. But for a few moments at least, we felt a tiny bit better.

After breakfast the next morning Lexie told me to dress like I was going to work. "I overheard Mom and Dad talking—the lawyer's coming at nine," she told me. "For the reading of the will."

"Are we allowed to be there?" It seemed like something for grown-ups.

"We're not going to ask," Lexie told me. "Sometimes it's better not to ask."

So I put on the cornflower-blue dress that you bought for me. And when the doorbell rang, I followed Lexie down the stairs and sat with her on the couch as my parents and Lexie's were all settling into seats.

Uncle Bob tried getting rid of us. "Why don't you girls go enjoy the sunshine?" he said in a big, hearty voice.

But Lexie looked at him very solemnly and said, "We're not interested in sunshine right now. This affects us, too, you know."

My parents were looking at me. "She's our grandmother," I told them.

There were lots of glances among the parents, and shrugs, and the lawyer was waiting kind of awkwardly, still standing near a chair, holding her briefcase.

Finally Uncle Bob said, "I guess that's fine." Then, to the lawyer, "Please, go ahead, have a seat."

The lawyer sat, and as she pulled documents out of her briefcase, she told us, "I'm not sure if any of you have seen this. But Ms. Gerta made changes about a week ago."

Everyone looked surprised.

"Only regarding the store," the lawyer said. She turned to Aunt Miriam. "She decided to leave it to Jacob and you. Instead of you alone."

Aunt Miriam took that in for one awkward second, and I thought, *Oh no!* I didn't want her to be angry—I didn't want more tension in the family. I wanted less. Much less.

But after that one second, she grinned at Dad. "I've always liked the idea of partnering with you."

He held up a hand and shook his head. "I don't think this changes anything, Miriam. Safta made her choice—she cut us off long ago. She can't just decide a week before she dies to rope us back in. We have a life in New York that we built because she rejected us. I want no part of the store."

"But you used to love running the store," Aunt Miriam said. "It was always your dream."

"Until it wasn't," Dad said.

I wanted so badly to interrupt him, tell him there were things he didn't know, things that might help him feel better about you, more understanding and forgiving. But I couldn't tell him—not yet. You'd only given me permission to share it with family, and the lawyer wasn't family.

While I was thinking all that, Mom slowed everything down.

"Let's take a little time and think about this. There are different ways we might be able to make something work."

The lawyer agreed that waiting made sense, then said some other things I didn't really pay attention to. I needed her to go.

When she finally did, I asked everyone to sit back down. "I have something to say, about Safta," I told them. "Please just listen—don't ask questions—it's going to be hard enough to get through."

They all listened without interrupting, until I got to Adelaide. Who you called Addy.

"Wait—hold on—are you saying Safta had a sister?" Aunt Miriam asked. "She never said a word about a sister. Are you sure?"

I nodded. "She was a few years older than Safta—about my age when the Nazis took her."

That's when Dad started to cry.

And then we all started to cry.

We held our first shiva later that day. (We held seven total, with the special yahrzeit candle always lit and the mirrors in Aunt Miriam's house covered with sheets and pillowcases. The way you would've wanted—the traditional Jewish way.)

We sat on Aunt Miriam's stiff living room furniture, balancing plates of food on our laps. Everyone took turns talking about you. Dad was beside me, on the sofa.

"As you all know, my mother and I had our troubles," he told everyone, sounding very awkward. "There's a lot I'm still trying to understand." He took my hand then. "I have good memories, though. Safta was the one who taught me how to tie a tie, and how to ballroom dance."

I liked imagining that last part—the two of you dancing fancy steps in your clean, white kitchen. You in an apron over a dress, maybe, about the age Mom is now. Dad in his cross-country uniform, a little older than me.

"Safta had funny theories about making friends at college, too. Remember?" Aunt Miriam asked Dad.

"'You must always keep good snacks in your room.'" Dad did a pretty bad imitation of you. Not nearly as good as Lexie's. "'Then people will come to see you.'"

They laughed together, and I could hear you so clearly in my mind saying, "They are laughing, but it is true, Catarina. You will go to college someday, and when you do, you must have plenty of treats for sharing. You will have friends then. You will see."

I like having you in my mind like that, bossing me around. Calling me Catarina.

In a few days we're heading back to New York. School will start soon, and Mom and Dad have to return to their jobs in Manhattan. But we'll be back in Baton Rouge before long. Dad's made arrangements with Aunt Miriam so we can help in the store during holidays like Christmas and over summers, too. Lexie tells me you bought an enormous mechanical Santa that sits on the roof of the store for weeks in December, rocking back and forth and shouting, "Ho, ho, ho, ho, ho!" I can't wait to see it.

It's funny to think of you, of all people, owning the largest Santa in Baton Rouge. I know what you'd say about that, though. "I provide the holiday decorations customers want. That doesn't mean I believe." It's like what you said about low-riding shorts and men's underwear: We don't have to wear them just because we stock them. From now on, that's what Santa's going to remind me of. Low-riding shorts and men's underwear.

Maybe I should be nervous about going back to school, since Blondie and Glitter will be there. I'm okay, though. What are they going to do? Run away from me? Pull out seats and put purses on them, to block me? Fine. I don't want to be near them anyway. Already Max is a way better friend than they ever were. I can't remember Amelia or Ruthie ever getting me something thoughtful when they knew I was feeling down. No smashable plates, and not even a single stick of gum (much less a lifetime supply).

Max makes me laugh a lot more than they ever did, too. I told him recently about Slick Billy and the Goatees, and he keeps texting me fake band names: "Pale Eddie and the Comb-Overs." "Plump Pete and the Man Buns." "Moist Mick and the Mullets."

I'm not going to have time to worry about Blondie and Glitter, anyway. I have a ton of Hebrew to learn. Mom and I are planning a bat mitzvah for me in the spring. When I bless the wine, I'm going to use the kiddush cup that your dad gave you when you boarded the boat from Germany. I'll put your prayer book on the bimah, too—the tattered one you liked to hold. I probably won't use it much, since it has no English. But it'll be there with me.

I want to keep writing my thoughts to you, too, the way I have since you died. I like thinking about what you would say or do, and what questions I'd ask you if I could. I like feeling close to you.

I have to make a confession, though: I don't always try to dress better, even though I know you want me to. I do wear the clothes you bought me, but only when I need to look especially good. The truth is, they're not as comfortable as my slouchy clothes. I don't enjoy being in them as much.

I'm not worrying about it, though. Because I've realized that maybe you're not as rigid as you used to seem. Take Lexie, for example. In your tough way, you always loved and took care of her, even though she snuck into her boyfriend's car, faked illnesses, made everyone think she'd been kidnapped when really she was snacking on bulk foods at the Piggly Wiggly, and never spent more than five minutes working in any department you ever assigned her to. You ultimately accepted my mom, too. And her religion is a much bigger deal than what I wear.

So I know it doesn't really matter whether my clothes ride too low or wash me out or need to be taken in. Even in mismatched seams, or too-small honey bear pajamas, I am still your Catarina.

Author's Note

When I was a girl, my family owned a department store on Main Street in Baton Rouge, Louisiana, around the corner from a cemetery. My grandparents had bought it with the savings they'd managed to smuggle out of Germany as they fled the Nazis in 1936. They had so little money left after buying the store, my grandfather told my grandmother they could afford a mop or a broom for the little apartment they'd rented nearby. Not both.

In its early days the store had wooden floors and a pot-bellied stove and only a few departments: men's and women's clothing, fabrics, and sewing supplies. Over the years it grew and grew. By the time I was born, it stretched over a full block. We sold candy and books and bikes and toys and perfumes and jewelry and curtains and bedspreads and shoes of every size.

On Saturday mornings when I was a girl, I went to work in the store. I'd tuck my blouse into my skirt, pin on my employee name tag, and pile into our wood-paneled station wagon with my siblings and our parents. After a five-minute drive we'd climb out at the store and head to our designated departments. I liked the idea of ringing up sales at a cash register, but I hated approaching strangers and asking if they needed help. I didn't like people paying attention to me, and I figured they might feel the same. Instead of even trying to sell, I'd slip behind a rack of blouses or display of purses and pretend to be straightening until I was sure no grown-up from my family was watching. Then I'd hurry to Books, hide in a back corner, and read until it was time to go home.

We lived across the street from my grandmother. (My grandfather, who'd fled Germany with her, died before I was born.) She helped run the store from the moment she arrived in Baton Rouge until the day more than fifty years later when we sold it, along with the other stores we'd opened. Under her reign, we'd built the largest family-owned department store chain in the country. She was a small woman, not much taller than five feet, and I always thought of her as ancient. But she was tough. We never called her Granny or Grandma. She insisted we use her first name: Lea. She told us exactly what she thought, always. I can still hear her voice, with its German accent: "That shirt is not flattering." "You've gained weight." "My cooking is better than your mother's cooking." (She was, in fact, a wonderful cook. Often she'd insist we eat her mouth-watering Southern fried chicken, for example, immediately after telling us we'd gained weight.)

Somehow, no matter what she said, her home always felt full of warmth. At the close of almost every day we'd cross the street and gather around her kitchen table. My aunts and uncles and cousins came, too—we all lived in walking distance of one another. Lea would set out tea and cookies, and the kids would listen as the grown-ups talked about issues at the store. Often the conversation would turn to our Jewish values and traditions, which Lea fiercely cherished, and to our family's past: the stores we'd owned in Germany; how Lea and her husband had escaped the Nazis with my dad and his siblings when they were little; and how they'd all built up the Baton Rouge store on Main Street until it was thriving. And so were we.

I've long wanted to write a book about a girl with a department store in Baton Rouge, a grandmother like Lea, and family roots in the calamity of 1930s Germany. *Summer of Stolen Secrets* is, finally, that book. I hope you enjoy it.